Sarah has been a master of the service industry most of her life. When she wakes on Imrahl, she is assigned to a position in a teashop with extra privileges as a courier. Six months of steady events go by, and then, her best friend and boss has a moment of evolution and lashes out.

Sarah wakes in the med centre and the minor empathy that had aided her all her life is now full-blow telepathy, and her mind is in danger.

Lekorh the Saya-Rrassic is the telepath of the colony, and he takes her under his care and, eventually, into his bed. She should have seen him coming, but she is a telepath, not a psychic.

Companion's Dilemma
Copyright © 2019 Viola Grace
ISBN: 978-1-4874-2472-5
Cover art by Angela Waters

Published by eXtasy Books Inc or
Devine Destinies, an imprint of eXtasy Books Inc

Look for us online at:
www.eXtasybooks.com or www.devinedestinies.com

COMPANION'S DILEMMA
BRACE FOR HUMANITY BOOK 5

BY

VIOLA GRACE

OTHER BOOKS IN THIS SERIES

CHAPTER ONE

Sarah yawned as she got out of her car and locked the door. The bakery's roof vent was already belching steam, but that was how it should be. The baker had been at his work for two hours.

Sarah fiddled with her keys as she crossed the lot, looking for the key to the front door. She had to open up in five minutes.

She could feel someone nearby, but there was always someone in a car waiting for the bakery to open so they could get the first donut of the day. When she felt the surge of their presence, she tried to turn, but there was a hiss, and her neck felt a cool pressure. She didn't see anyone, and then, everything went black.

She was breathing, but there wasn't air. She could feel people near her, but it was like they were all asleep and neatly arranged. There were other folk nearby, but she couldn't get a grip on how they thought. They were pillars of self-control moving through the ranks of sleeping people.

She closed her eyes, and when she woke up again, the feeling of a few days passing was evident. The minds of the other humans were changing. They were being taken out of their confinement, and something was being added to them. Their minds, their auras were changing while her mind watched.

Sarah had never thought about how she sensed things before, but she had plenty of time to consider it. Normally, her senses were linked to body language as well as the person's general energy vibe. But wherever she was now, she didn't even need her eyes to see. She was sensing from inside a fluid suspension and waiting for one of the humans she was watching to experience something unpleasant.

She listened with her mind and only found that the minds were being given something extra. To her surprise, she was listening to the others so intently that when she was grabbed, she flailed a little.

They fished her out, and mild sedation was applied. Her limbs went floppy. She was turned to one side and her lungs and stomach emptied of fluid rather violently. When she was breathing normally, she was laid back on the gurney for the next procedure.

Careful fingers opened her eyes, and the sudden influx of light blinded her. Information began to stream in through the lenses, and now, she understood what the others had received. They were getting an alien language and the rudiments of society.

She felt hands drying her, and then, they dressed her flopping and useless limbs. They obviously had practice as even her bra was smoothed into place with the ease of practice. When she was completely covered by what she could tell was her uniform, they wheeled her into the room where the other humans were being prepped, and her headset was still in place.

Information was streaming through the unit, and she kept herself open to anything it wanted to tell her. The language she was receiving was Rrassic common. It was the language given to all the species that the Rrassic abducted. She was there to help in their war effort.

Sarah didn't know what kind of help she would be. She was content to sell muffins for a living. She sighed and kept still as the language nuances continued to fill into her thoughts.

The minds around her fell into the rhythms of sleep, and the efficient alien minds started to move through the rows of sleeping humans. Hands carefully removed the lens unit on her, and she didn't know how to pretend she was asleep. She blinked rapidly, and a man in pale grey smiled down at her. His face was vaguely feline, and his skin was a soft dove grey.

He inclined his head and murmured, "Welcome to Imrahl, little one."

She didn't know why he called her little until she saw the headset in his hands. *Oh. That's why.* He was larger than she was by close to two feet in height, and she had no idea how much wider at the shoulders he was.

She rolled the words in her mouth and whispered in Rrassic common. "Thank you?"

He grinned and stroked her cheek. "Get some rest, lass. You will need it."

She closed her eyes and tried to calm her mind. Sarah breathed evenly of the air with unfamiliar scents and let herself drift off. At least she wasn't alone.

She sat across from a cheerfully polite woman who checked her file. "So, you work at a bakery?"

"I did. Yes. I am counter personnel."

The woman smiled. "Do you like it?"

"I do. I like working with people."

"Good. There are a few positions for you. You can work at a teashop or as a courier or both if you are so inclined."

"A courier?"

"Yes, delivering the clothing from tailors to secure areas. You don't have any inclination for violence, so I am willing to put you up for a high security clearance."

Sarah smiled and looked at the woman who was wearing

the name Isabella in her mind loud and proud. She delved in slightly and blinked as a bit of information emerged. Her smile wobbled. "I think I would like to start at the teashops and go from there."

"Very well, I will still put in for your security clearance. You never know when something will come up."

The wristband was printed, and Sarah extended her arm. The click of it as it closed on her wrist had a certain finality. "Right, so where do I go from here?"

"There is a kiosk outside that has your address in it. Just use the scanners, and they will tell you where you work, how to get there, and how to find your way. Orientation sessions will be had in your building, and it should be fine in no time. Bear with them. The Rrassic don't really mean us any harm."

Sarah got to her feet. "I understand. It's okay. I will be my own little cog in this machine, and hopefully, I won't ruffle any feathers or fur or whatever they have."

Isabella smiled. "Fur. They all have a fine nap of fur."

"Good to know. I hope that I see you around."

Isabella nodded. "I hope the same. Have a good day."

Sarah smiled again and headed out of the office and toward the front of the building where other sorted humans were standing, waiting for their turn at the machines.

Sarah hummed softly and worked around the edge of the crowd, peeping outside. She saw a scan unit out on the street next to a shop, and she shrugged, leaving her people behind and walking up to the unit to scan her band.

She grinned. She lived three blocks north and two blocks east. Her job was one block west of her home.

With a casual look around, she walked out with her hands in her uniform pockets, and she smiled and nodded at the few men that she passed on the street. She kept her trepidation to herself. This was where she lived, and she knew why she was here. Isabella's mind had been very forthright. They weren't the original women that had been taken, they were clones in the clothing of the original.

Somewhere on Earth, Sarah Wilkerson had been set down bare ass naked. She would not be pleased.

She smiled at the thought that somewhere out there her own personality had gone from frightened to furious in a matter of heartbeats. Once trustworthy people were around her, she would have calmed right down. It would have been a weird anecdote for her to recount when she was with friends on a Friday night.

As Sarah walked through the streets, she saw a few more information kiosks and made a note of the location in case she got lost.

In a fit of whimsy, she walked to the teashop before she went to her apartment.

The shop was occupied by several Rrassic sitting around and eating a surprising array of cakes with their tea. She grinned. She was going to have to learn these things.

She walked up to the counter and looked at the silvery male behind it. "Hello. I am Sarah Wilkerson. I believe that this is my place of work?"

She felt all the heads of the men in the shop turn toward her.

The man—she looked for the specific definition and found it—Nool looked at her with a smile. "I was not expecting you until tomorrow. Come in the back, and I will show you around. I am Vedder, and I own this teashop."

She smiled. "Please. I am here to learn."

He walked her through the washing station, the serving station, and the dessert layout as well as some savoury pastries. There was a selection of thirty items that she would have to remember.

"Why did you come so early?"

She shrugged. "I skipped going to my apartment. The crowd won't work itself out for an hour or more. I can usually find my way around with a map."

"You found a map?"

"My assessment officer told me about the kiosks. I wanted to see if they worked. They really do."

Vedder chuckled. "I am glad you have sense. I was terrified that they would send me a bit of fluff that needed protecting."

"I might need a hand if they get grabby, but from what my initial programming tells me, I am fairly safe here."

She looked at him. "What time do you need me tomorrow?"

"An hour before dawn. We cater to the early shift coming on and the late shift getting off."

"And how long do I work?"

"We cease operations mid-afternoon. There are other shops open all day, but I have never felt it necessary."

Sarah smiled. "I think that will be fine. So, is there a listing for what the pastries are?"

"No, they are all traditional Rrassic foods. Look up pastries when you get to your quarters tonight, and tomorrow, you will be given samples before you start."

She nodded. "I will. What about the teas?"

"The teas are all listed on the menu. You can read Rrassic common?"

She stared at the glyphs, and they moved into an understandable format. "Apparently."

She looked down at her uniform. "What about clothing?"

"Wear something comfortable that won't get caught on anything." Vedder grinned. "That is good for today. I will see you tomorrow. Get your rest, this place bustles in the morning."

"Wait. One more thing. How do folks pay, and how do I

ring it up?"

He blinked. "Oh, right."

He showed her the system that was simply push button and swipe the wristband. Everything was done with the band.

She cheerfully declined nine offers to walk her to her quarters and walked out to her apartment building. The wristband allowed her access, and she joined the gathering of nervous women in the lobby for the full orientation.

The scaly Rrassic representative looked relieved when she appeared on his roster via her scan in, and he took them on a tour of their facilities. The other women were radiating fear and nervousness, so Sarah kept away from them when she could. She didn't know what had set her mind off, but it was picking up far too much ambient emotion. Working in the tea house was going to be easy. Lust was excellent to dodge. It didn't follow you, it simply radiated.

When she got to her apartment, she closed the door with relief and went to make herself a cup of coffee. She pulled up short when she realized that there wasn't any coffee to be had. *Damn.* She was in hell after all.

CHAPTER TWO

Sarah took her tray around and picked up the teacups and plates that had been left behind. Vedder was preparing for the lunch rush, and only the late-shift regulars were still hanging around.

She took the dishes to the back and set them in the cleanser. "Well, Vedder, it has been six months. What do you think of having a human assistant?"

He grinned. "I think that I could have a full-time baker on staff and still not keep up. I don't know what you do to the customers but keep it up."

She grinned. "I just listen and help them with flirting tips for wooing humans."

She reset as much as she could and went out to chat with the last three Rrassic who were in her café.

Eegan, the Zjin, leaned toward her. "Sarah, why don't you let me take you away from all this and worship you for hours on end?"

Sarah grinned. "Because it is the middle of my shift, and by the time I am free, you will have gotten off all on your own."

His buddies laughed.

He sighed. "You are exceptionally cruel."

"That is why I work here. Anything else for you, Rokin, Melor?" The Regiz and Luthin shook their heads. Their Hunter team often came in after a late night doing whatever it was they did. Their blend of varieties of Rrassic was rare in a team. There tended to be one Zjin and the other members of the team were of another type, but these three got along very well.

They shook their head, and Rokin answered, "We are good. Thanks for letting us decompress here."

"It is Vedder's place. I just work here." She picked up their spent dishes and put them on her tray.

"See you tomorrow, Sarah. Stay cheerful." Eegan nodded, and the other two bowed slightly.

She did a clear out at high speed and got the teashop ready for the rush. Only fourteen people could be seated in the shop at a time, but the takeout option was always there. The tea was served in paper cups that only lasted ten hours once hot liquid had been added. It was a devious idea that Sarah definitely admired. Of course, it meant that if you took some home and didn't drink it, you were going to have a large puddle where your tea used to be.

When the first of the lunch rush arrived, she got to work, and before she knew it, she was approaching the end of the day. She finished up the dishes and took a look at what was left in the display.

"Vedder, can I take what's left?"

He was frowning and rubbing his forehead. "Sure. Yes. Sorry. I have been a little distracted lately."

She smiled and patted his arm. "Take care of yourself."

"I will." He paused. "Sarah?"

She was getting her delivery bag ready, and she stopped to make eye contact. "What is it, Vedder?"

"Would you be upset if I changed?"

Sarah set the bag aside and went over to take his hand. "You are my friend. You can physically change all you like, but I am going to remain at your disposal."

Understanding flared in his eyes. "You know."

"I do. I know what to expect. Will you be gone long, or will you ever be back?"

He dragged in a deep breath. "I will be back as soon as I can, but I am turning into a Zjin, so there will be complications to my transformation. I will be expected to take on a commanding role."

She nodded. "You are good at being bossy. Just channel it into your work. Will you be closing the teashop?"

"No. I have requested another Nool to take over running the shop and the baking, but you will have to keep him on the right path."

She nodded. "I will." She wiped a tear from her cheek. "Right. I am going to take the pastry to the admin building and then work my way through the city."

It was a way for her to move things through the marketplace without gathering attention. She had delivered quite a few tailored bits of clothing to ladies in the Breeder compound as discreetly as she could.

The first stop was the admin building, so she walked the route and entered the main floor, scanning her wrist at the lift to get up to the overseer's offices. She had the pack in one hand, and when she left the lift, she looked around to see if she could locate Isabella.

The giggle from the overseer's office tipped Sarah off. She went to Isabella's desk and got out the two pastries that were the favourite for the assistant and her mate. Steeling herself for the emotional onslaught, she took the two wrapped articles and walked them into the overseer's office, setting them on the desk before she turned and walked away.

Isabella gasped, and Iktabi laughed, but Sarah kept moving.

Sarah blocked them both out and closed up her pack. She had one more stop on this floor, and she would be on her regular rounds.

She paused outside Lekorh's office and knocked. She

didn't need to. He knew she was there.

"Come in."

She opened the door and stepped inside the dim office. Lekorh was kneeling with a glowing stone mounted in the wall in front of him. His third eye was open and staring into that light.

It would have been less disturbing if Lekorh had been wearing more than trousers. His shining grey skin and golden hair made him look like he was carved of metal. The design on his skin had to be some sort of tattoo, but she had never heard of tattoos on Rrassic before.

"What are you in the mood for today?" She bit her lip as soon as she said it. Her fascination with his physique hadn't diminished since she first saw him two months prior.

His lips curved in a slight smile, and he got to his feet. "What do you have to offer?"

She squelched her focus on his abs and opened the pack. "A little of everything."

He stood next to her and peered into the bag. "One of the cream buns and one of the cheesecakes."

She blinked. He always chose the ones that she had made as if he knew. She sighed and reached in; he probably had read it in her thoughts. Passive information was something that he picked up on, and the Saya-Rrassic couldn't help it.

She set the treats on small napkins, and she raised her gaze to meet his. "On the desk?"

He smiled slowly.

Her mind was filled with an intimate image of her lying back across the desk while he parted her thighs.

She stifled the image and smiled at him. "Desk or do you wear them for that little stunt."

He laughed. "On the desk is fine. I have another hour of meditation to get through."

He didn't admit to inserting that image in her thoughts,

and to be honest, she couldn't be sure that it wasn't her own work. She set the pastries down on his desk. Sarah packed up her bag and closed it. "Serene meditation to you."

He nodded and returned to his spot on the cushion he had on the floor. "I will see you soon, Sarah."

There was an implicit threat in his tone. She grabbed her bag and left his office without looking behind her. When the door was closed, she exhaled slowly, and she could swear that she heard a peal of laughter from behind the door.

She recorded the sales in her portable tablet, and the administration accounts paid out. She went to the floor below and wandered through each of the offices, offering the Rrassic and the human administrators some of the pastries before she finished making her way through the building.

Sarah had half a dozen pastries left, so she headed to the market. The tailor that she was heading for had been supplying some of the new and exotic workout gear for the human women. There was one lady mated to a Zjin, and Sarah had heard a whisper that there was going to be a human presence in the peacekeeping occupation.

All rumours ran through the teashop, and she kept her ears and mind open.

She walked into the marketplace and smiled at a few other humans as she went. The clothing shop was quiet, and she entered it with a smile. "Yoris, I have some pastries if you are interested."

The massive Nool came out, and he grinned. "Anything savoury today?"

She peeped in her collection. "Three wrapped eggs, two poultry envelopes."

"Can I have them all? I skipped lunch."

She nodded and brought up the bill. He swiped his band, and she unpacked her food onto the tray he provided. The food was whisked to the back, and she closed up her pack.

He brought out a folded pack. "These are really popular. I need this sent to Niiva at the Breeder compound."

She placed the pack under her bag and pressed down. The secret compartment folded around the parcel and the pack disappeared.

"I will take it. Anything else?"

Yoris looked her over. "You are looking a little worn. Maybe a new tunic and leggings for you?"

She looked down at what she would have called a long-sleeved t-shirt dress. "What is wrong with this?"

"You should wear more colour."

She was wearing blocks of black and grey on her dress. "Why? This lets me do my job."

Yoris sighed. "There is more to life than jobs."

"I know, but I haven't found out what there is yet." She grinned. "I will see you tomorrow."

He blinked. "Are you empty?"

"Of course. I saved the last five savouries for you. See you tomorrow."

She left with her hidden burden and walked back to her apartment building where she got her cycle. Having her own independent transport was one of her favourite parts of the delivery-person job. It got her an extra few credits per day and let her go out and see the countryside that was open for viewing.

She got onto her cycle and activated it. The parcel was strapped on the back, and her helmet was in place. Sarah entered the street with its sparse traffic and headed for the outer limits of the city where the Breeders were separated from the rest of the population.

The edge of the city gave way to wilderness for a few minutes, but then, she was pulling up to one of the most secure facilities on Imrahl.

She pulled up at the gate. "Delivery."

The guard looked at her, and she removed her helmet. She extended her band, and he scanned it.

"Proceed." She nodded and drove through the gate after she put her helmet on. Safety first.

She parked and removed the parcel from her bag. She tucked it under her arm and kept the helmet on.

A scan at the door gave her Niiva's address, so she headed up the steps with her helmet still on.

Her scan at the main door had shown her that Niiva was not in the building, so Sarah was free to walk up to her door and use her clearance to enter Niiva's private quarters to drop off the clothing. She folded the underwear and placed it in the wardrobe before leaving the apartment as silently as she had entered it.

It was part of her after-hours work that she was able to walk into any level of any building in Imrahl. She wore the helmet to keep her anonymity. If any of these ladies saw her in the city, she didn't want to be questioned about what she had been delivering. Frankly, it was none of their business.

CHAPTER THREE

Vedder's approach to transformation made the teashop a little tense. The replacement baker was good, but there was a little more resistance to the human delicacies than she had been counting on.

Sarah was out front discussing traditional pastries with one of their customers when she heard a tremendous crack from the kitchen.

Vedder was standing there, his muscles twitching and a deep blue colouration under his skin in definite stripes.

"Vedder, what is it?" She reached out to touch him, and he swatted her away.

Sarah flew through the air and thudded into the wall, smacking her head rather hard. The patrons from the shop ran in and confined her friend.

Eegan had control of Vedder. Melor helped him ease Vedder out the door.

Rokin touched the back of Sarah's head, and he winced. "You both are going to medical."

Sarah grunted. "Sommin, the new baker. He was here before the noise."

Rokin quickly looked around the table. "He's out cold."

"Make sure he isn't dead, get some more help from out front, and call some transport medics." She was clutching her head.

Rokin did a quick triage, and Sommin groaned and got to his feet, clutching his jaw.

Rokin nodded and said, "Close shop and report to

medical."

Sommin nodded. "Yes, Hunter."

Sarah asked, "Are you okay, Sommin?"

She swayed, and Rokin caught her.

Sommin lunged toward her. "What happened?"

Rokin headed for the front of the shop with her in his arms. "She tried to intercede on your behalf. Vedder lost control."

Sommin nodded, scowled, and followed them to the door.

Sarah felt that everything was in hand, so she let herself pass out.

The med centre was usually calm, but she heard shouting from down the hall, and it was not helping her headache. She glanced at the scanners and checked the time. She had lost six hours.

Sarah sighed and tried to feel for the people around her, and her sense took a sudden surge.

She found her friend's mind in a riot of hot hormones, and she decided to intervene. *"Vedder! Calm the fuck down!"*

She felt his senses grapple with her presence, and he began to slowly cycle to a normal state. His final maturation into a Zjin had begun, and it was going to be stressful. Thankfully, Vedder already had the physique that the Zjin were known for.

Her skull throbbed, and she pulled the monitor over to where she could bring up the details of what had happened. Sarah's skull had cracked, and she had ruptured blood vessels in her brain. If she hadn't gotten immediate treatment, she would have been dead. The portions of her brain that had been exposed to blood were no longer properly functioning, and with stimulation, her brain had begun to reroute its function.

"Damn it."

She felt a cool sensation in her mind, and she looked away from the monitor to see a hooded figure in her doorway.

She cocked her head. "Lekorh?"

He stepped into the room and walked toward the bed. "When you did not arrive for your customary delivery, I knew that something had happened. I have been waiting for you to wake. How are you feeling?"

"Like my head was boxed with." She grimaced.

"May I?" He held out his hand.

"Um, sure."

Lekorh moved in close, and he ran his hand through her pixie-cut hair. Wherever he touched, a cool relief ran through her skull.

She leaned into his touch and asked, "Why did you come here?"

"I heard you, so I was here as fast as I could be."

"Heard me?"

"Yes, you are rather noisy in the psychic sense."

She could see the outline of his smile in the shadow of his hood.

His hand was her favourite thing in the world right now.

He chuckled. "I know."

She looked toward where his eyes should be. "Can you go and see Vedder? He isn't doing well."

He grinned. "You told him to *'calm the fuck down.'* That seems to have had an effect."

"I just yelled at him. You can actually do something. Don't worry about me. I will be fine."

Lekorh kept his hand on her skull. "You are still in pain."

She sighed. "And he is in agony. I am doing triage. Please, go and see him."

Lekorh eased her back to the bed and took the monitor away. "None of this until I return."

She nodded and closed her eyes. She felt the soft brush of

lips against hers, but before she could open her eyes, he was gone.

She counted the number of people in the med centre, and she hoped that the sixty-three people who were in the building were having a better night than she was.

"Sarah Wilkerson, you are awake." The Nool medic smiled.

"I am. Is Vedder all right?"

"Saya Lekorh is helping him now. How are you feeling?"

"Sore. A bit battered but otherwise fine. I am more concerned about Vedder."

"You should be concerned for yourself. You nearly died. Your brain had ruptured vessels, and we patched up what we could, but it is unknown if you will recover full function."

She held up her hands and flexed them. "My coordination is fine."

"The monitors will tell us how you are actually doing. You are no judge of your own health."

Sarah blinked in surprise. She tried to touch the Nool's mind and was exposed to a fascinating situation. "Sommin still has a job if he wants it. He just has to accept that there are also human clients and Rrassic who want insight into humans via their food. If he wants to put in the work, I want his help to keep the teashop as one of the highest earners for the snack shops."

Medic Cwin blinked and stopped in place. "How do you know that?"

"I just know." She sought out Sommin's mind in the med centre, and she found him, wallowing in regret. "Tell him that things are fine. Vedder is adjusting to his transformation."

The medic looked at her with wide eyes. "Your brain. There is no register for this activity."

She gave him a bland look. "They are looking for Rrassic brain waves. It has taken me months, but now, I can move my mind between the species."

A shadow moved behind him, and Cwin froze in place. She felt the last few minutes leaving his mind and a more benign concern for Sommin taking hold.

The medic left her room, and Sarah was pretty sure that he didn't remember her.

Lekorh walked into the room. "You can't remain here."

She frowned. "Okay. Great. Where do I go while recovering from a cracked skull?"

He stepped toward her and touched her forehead gently. She felt cool darkness surround her, and everything went soft and black.

Recognizing minds was something new, but they were too far for her to hear their voices, so she simply listened in.

Isabella was perturbed. "You stole her."

Iktabi was wary of his mate, so he wasn't saying anything.

Lekorh sighed. "I stole her. Her mind has awakened, and she is seeking out other minds." His voice got stern. "She is wrecking privacy and breaking protocols the moment she wakes. Her brain is a new shiny toy, and she is playing with it."

"Geez, Lekorh, why are you shouting?"

"So that Sarah will listen to my words. She is awake and listening in."

Sarah blinked and she sat up in bed. They were coming her way.

Lekorh came in first, and behind him were Iktabi and Isabella with a physician behind them. Dr. Lem. He was a Sthik-Rrassic, and his serpentine gaze was fixed on her when he came through the doorway.

She waved to the group. "Hello. Sorry this is creating such a fuss."

The physician came to her and sat at the edge of her bed. "Hello, Sarah."

"Hello, Dr. Lem."

The gasp that came from Isabella echoed the shock in Iktabi's mind and the smugness in Lekorh's.

"So, you have been listening in to conversations." Dr. Lem smiled and took out a scanner. He pressed two pods to her temples, and he continued to ask her questions. "What do you last remember before waking up?"

"Lekorh put me to sleep."

"Before that?"

She blinked. "He undid something that I did to Cwin."

"What did you do to him?"

"I told him that I could read his thoughts, and then, I found Sommin in the med centre and read all of his insecurity and guilt. I told Cwin to go to him and reassure him."

Lekorh's mind was bristling with the rush of vindication.

She gave him a look, and his mind stilled, and a silvery curtain covered his thoughts. "That is neat."

He smiled and nodded for her to keep speaking to Dr. Lem. It was hard to answer what he was asking and not what he was thinking.

"Why aren't you shocked by your new situation?"

She looked at the scaled Rrassic. "I have always had some touch with those around me. It makes me a better server. I can deflect or deflate irritating clients. Of course, now, that would be bad. I see too much. Damn. I am going to need another job."

Her forthright answers were coming from the small pods. They were acting as a mild intoxicant and taking away the care she normally took with her speech.

She frowned at the doctor, and he smiled. "You are also a

quick study. Excellent intuition."

He sat back. "Now, tell me what you have learned since I sat down."

She ticked things off her fingers, "Isabella is pregnant again, Iktabi is hoping that the flight didn't take because he wanted to do it again. Lekorh can put a muffler on his mind, and you were requested by Lekorh to do an assessment on me because he has been sensing my awakening for the last few months."

She looked at Dr. Lem. "You are a psychic specialist who wrote a monograph on finding Saya in other species. Your theory is that every species develops a version of those who are mind-sighted. You also have interviewed Lekorh for a number of other articles as you two were decanted on the same day and share a genetic donor. Huh. You are brothers."

She looked at the folks surrounding her. "More?"

Lekorh shook his head. "That is enough. Dr. Lem?"

Lem grinned. "That is fine. I will remove the inhibitors, but I will say, you operate on a frequency that we can't even measure. Lekorh can feel it, but I didn't feel a thing. I thought he was nuts at first, but there is no doubting that you have the ability to pull deep details out of a Rrassic."

She blinked at the use of the word *nuts* in his expression. "You aren't stationed here, but you use our phrasing. Ah, you were on an assessment team embedded on Earth to figure out how we work as a society. You designed Imrahl to match an average of what you found."

Lekorh stated, "Sarah, stop."

She looked at him, and his eyes locked with her gaze. All three of his eyes. She felt the cool touch on her mind, and it soothed the bits that had gotten overheated.

Lekorh sat on the other side of the bed, and he cupped her head as he soothed all the pieces of her mind that had burning embers in it. "Easy, Sarah. You are pulling too hard."

Dr. Lem cleared his throat. "Well, I can confirm that she has Saya skills. Will you send me reports, Lekorh?"

"Yes, Lem."

Isabella cleared her throat. "What do you need from us?"

Lekorh smiled. "Privacy and a few changes of clothing for her until we can arrange something a little more formal."

Iktabi nodded. "How far do you need us?"

Sarah whispered, "It doesn't matter. I can hear them all."

Lekorh blinked. "All?"

"Right up to the baby in gestation tube four. The other ones aren't thinking yet."

Isabella's shock coasted across her mind.

Lekorh lifted his head and said, "Everyone out. She can't stop, and I need to begin immediate instruction."

She wasn't sure what he meant until she felt her mind unravelling as it touched and learned from every mind on Imrahl. She was losing herself, and it was happening fast.

Chapter Four

The kiss shocked her. Her feeling of drifting away via other people's minds was suddenly gone, and her entire focus was on Lekorh and the shivers of pleasure that she was experiencing.

When Lekorh lifted his head, he had a serious expression. "Are you with me?"

She nodded. "I am back. The drifting has stopped."

His lips had a shine on them, and his third eye was wide open. She smiled apologetically. "I am sorry. I should have pulled it together."

He stroked her hair and cupped her head in both hands. "You are doing exceptionally well. My own awakening was dangerous for all those around me. At least you are not known to the population."

She nodded. "Aside from all of my regulars. They will be looking for me. They are worried."

He sighed. "Right. You were involved with the public. I will speak with Vedder and Sommin. We will get a new server in place."

She grumbled. "At least tell me I can still be a courier."

"Only if you learn to conceal your presence from others. That will take some time."

He was still close to her, and she looked up at his eyes and then looked away. "I think I am safe for now."

"Relatively. The moment your curiosity sparks, your mind will take off."

He leaned back and sighed. She didn't try to rummage into his mind, but it was a close thing.

"Well done. Knowing that you could look but shouldn't is the first step. Now, get up and take a shower. By the time you are dry, a change of clothing will be on the way."

He disappeared while she sat there. She reached out with her hand, but he wasn't there. She fought the urge to look for him and carefully got out of the bed.

There were small knickknacks on shelves on the walls. The bed was sized for a Rrassic. She was in Lekorh's bedroom, but she had no idea what part of the city she was actually in.

Why the kiss? He had kissed her to reset her mind, and she didn't know why it worked.

She moved around the room and eventually found the door of the bathing room next to that of the lav. Having the two rooms separate was handy and way less creepy than she had initially imagined. She had heard of them around the world, but her North American upbringing had never prepared her for the practicality.

She first attended to a call of nature, and then, she headed over to the bathing room.

She stripped to the skin and warmed the water in the shower. The bath was tempting, but it had not been offered as an option.

The light rain of the warm water came down from the ceiling, and she stood with her arms raised above her head while curls of pink water headed for the drain. Her head had really taken a knock.

The shampoo came out of the dispenser, just like it did in her own quarters, but there was absolutely no scent to it. The soap was the same. There was no scent to anything regarding cleansing, but she could smell the water.

Once she had finished gingerly washing the new skin on the back of her skull, she turned off the shower and stepped out, wrapping herself in a drying cloth. Since it was sized for Lekorh, it fit easily around her, and she tucked it in over her breasts.

When she emerged from the slightly steamy bathing room, the bed had been made, and there was no sign that she had been in there to start with.

She turned behind her and went to grab her clothing, but her outfit was gone. A quick look showed her that the clothing refresher was lit up and working on something, so she guessed that her clothing was all going through a cycle.

She licked her lips and felt thirsty, which prompted her to go looking for water. She left the bedroom and walked into the main area of the apartment, looking for windows or anything that would give her an idea of where she was.

She saw something glitter out of the corner of her eye, and she walked toward a window that showed an expanse that shocked her. The city was over five miles away, and she was at a vantage point, looking over them. "How high are we?"

She couldn't sense him, but she knew Lekorh was there.

"We are in the mountainside. No one can approach us without going through nine layers of security and then requesting entrance." He walked up behind her, and he looked at their reflection in the window.

"How did we get here?"

"I carried you from the med centre to the rail system, and it brought us here. I had to let the others in because Dr. Lem has been curious about you since I first mentioned you months ago."

"Months?" She smiled.

"Months. Since the day you first came into the administration offices and offered Isabella sugar in the middle of the board meeting."

Sarah smiled. "It worked. I was allowed to get all of the

offices involved."

"How did you know she was hungry?"

Sarah looked back at him. "I watched to see how many of the staff came out for snacks and at which time. Yes, I stalked the building."

"That explains the confidence you had with everyone's selections."

"All except you. I would never have pegged you for a human-dessert fellow."

He shrugged. "Reading minds burns a lot of calories."

She sighed. "I find it is *not* reading them that is causing the problem at the moment."

"You will learn how to keep things out." He sighed. "Do you want to know what is going to happen?"

She blinked. "Sure."

"Let's have a seat."

He led her over to a low table where a cushion was going to act as her seat. "Apologies. I don't actually entertain, so this is what I use for eating meals and watching vids."

She blushed. "Right. Apologies."

She cinched her wrap a little tighter and slowly knelt on the cushion. He got another one out and got some tea from a sideboard before returning with two cups and the pot. She didn't care. She was so thirsty she would take whatever was provided.

He poured the tea, and she accepted her cup, sipping at it as soon as she could. Her dry mouth absorbed the first sip, and she continued to drink in slow increments.

Every time she set it down, he refilled it without speaking. She kept her mind occupied replaying the kiss, and when her body started reacting to the memory, she had to stop. Finally, she asked, "So, what is going to happen next?"

He smiled. "What is going to happen is what just happened. You used the memory of the kiss to pull yourself back into your own mind. The mind-body connection is key to keeping control of what you can and can't do."

He sighed. "Or rather should and shouldn't."

She nodded. "I understand. I knew there had to be a reason for the kiss."

Lekorh gave her a strange look. "We will get into that later. For now, you are now officially my companion. This will allow you to travel with me, and I can monitor your progress and control at all times."

"What if I am not with you?"

He gave her a look. "You will be here or somewhere else secure."

She sighed. "I don't deal well with confinement."

"It will only be until you get control of your mind. As for the instruction you are about to undergo, it has already begun."

She nodded, and her stomach growled aggressively.

He bit his lips. "Or, perhaps we should have something to eat."

She smiled though she was blushing. "That would probably be a good thing."

He gracefully rose to his feet, the long outer vest swung, and she watched him glide across the space and into the kitchen.

Lekorh pulled out the ingredients for a meal, and to her horror, he started to cook.

He glanced at her. "You don't cook?"

"No. I have worked in food service my whole life. I eat at work or bring food home."

"Come sit over here and begin to learn. As my companion, you will be responsible for my body during periods of uninterrupted work." He smiled.

"You have to be kidding. I can't even keep a plant alive."

"I will request what I need when I need it. You need only

acquire it for me."

He smiled and minced and sliced his way into a nice-looking stir fry. He glanced back at her. "I know you provided the human recipes for Vedder's café."

She shrugged. "I provided the recipes, he put them together. I never had to lift a finger. I don't think Sommin will be as charitable."

"He is insecure, and it gave him an unfortunate reaction. I have spoken with him, and he will listen to you if you advise him on what is most popular with which clients."

"So, he lipped off, and Vedder lost it."

"Pretty much. It was a short argument that ended when Vedder ended it. Sommin should not have been goading him. He is far enough from his own transformation to know what will happen eventually, and he should have treaded more carefully."

"So, it is Sommin who is to blame?"

He shrugged and dished out food on a single platter. "If you know that prodding a dangerous but friendly member of society is going to set them off, would you do it?"

"Of course not."

"Well, he did. He knew it would happen, he forced it anyway."

She nodded and got a flicker from him of where the water decanter and glasses were located. Sarah smiled. "Isn't telling me like that cheating?"

"No. Not if it makes your stomach quiet."

She sighed. "I haven't eaten since breakfast, and my body has been through a bit."

"Understandable."

She set the water vessel down on the small table and arranged the cups as Lekorh had indicated. He brought the stir fry over and set it down in the centre of the table.

Fortunately, he had two sets of eating prongs. Only two.

She knelt and then slammed a hand to her chest as her wrap loosened. "Yikes."

"Your clothing may have finished its cycle. This will keep for a few minutes."

She kept her hand on the connection of the wrap, got to her feet, and headed back into what appeared to be the only bedroom.

The cycle had completed, so she quickly got dressed in her long tunic. The rest of the clothing could wait until later. She was hungry.

She returned to the living space with bare legs after setting the towel into the cleaning cycle and wadding her clothes into a pile.

Lekorh smiled and nodded. "Better?"

"I think you have seen enough of me for the day, so yes."

"We will discuss that as well. I only have one bed, and I require my sleep, so you can either join me there or make up a bed out here for the night."

She reached out and took some of the meat and vegetable. "I will think about it."

"Well, tonight, you will sleep in my bed. You need monitoring after your injury."

She nodded. "Even humans have the injured party monitored for a day. Of course, they also make you wake up on the hour to make sure that you are not in a coma."

She ate, and he ate. Their meal was in peculiar silence as she was used to noise around her at all times. Even the roar of her cycle was a sound that she was used to.

The quiet of eating made her mindful of each bite, and she ate, swallowed, and tried to make as little sound as possible. The food was good, if a bit bland, and when the meal was finished, she collected the dishes without prompting. Cleaning up after diners was something she was familiar with.

Lekorh moved the table to one side, and he pulled their

cushions closer together. "When you are done, we will work on your focus."

She nodded and dispatched the dishes into the cleaning units, cleaned up everything in the sink, and set the entire kitchen back the way it had been.

When she returned to the cushion, she knelt, and Lekorh extended his hands, palms up. She placed her hands in his and closed her eyes.

The cool wash of his thoughts over hers made her smile, and soon, he was guiding her on a careful look through the world of Imrahl, and it had nothing to do with the city.

CHAPTER FIVE

"How long have you known that you were grown?"

She answered him on what had to be the psychic plane, but it looked like an empty city in the middle of Imrahl. She would not normally be standing naked in the middle of the street, but today was not a normal day.

She looked at Lekorh, and he was wearing the same outfit that she was. There was a lot more of him to see, but his body seemed fairly casual about it.

Sarah kept her gaze straight ahead. "I woke up in the canister. I could feel folks around me, sleeping. The alert minds didn't quite emote like the ones I was used to, but they did seem very concerned about their charges."

"Good. But you have kept it to yourself this entire time?"

"I have. Well, I shared Isabella's knowledge. She has a really open mind."

He snorted. "Tell me about it. She broadcasts like an emergency tower, and I don't have the heart to tell her that I can hear everything she does."

Sarah winced. "At close proximity, that must be rough."

"You will learn all about it when we are working in the admin office."

She shuddered. "I will have a word with her. Since Iktabi flirts with her constantly, it must be like watching a tame S&M film."

"What is that?"

She gave him an image of a man pulling a tether tight and then wrapping it around his fist, bringing his female toward

31

him.

He cleared his throat. "Very apt."

"Thanks. It got into my head that first day and hasn't left it. So, Lekorh, why are we here?"

"We are here for you to practice your overlay skills."

"I don't have any skills."

"Humour me. Move to any place in the city and tell me what the occupants are thinking about."

That seemed easy enough, but the place she wanted to be wasn't occupied. She went to the teashop anyway.

She was surrounded by Rrassic. Close to a dozen. "They shouldn't be here."

She listened, and the plan she heard chilled her.

Lekorh put his hands on her shoulders. "Just listen to their surface minds. Listen to what they say."

Sarah listened to their thoughts, and she wasn't happy about it.

"What do you hear?"

"They are planning to grab some of the human women at the concert tomorrow."

He spoke softly. "Where are they going to take them?"

"Rohadda. The portal is going to be at the northeast corner of the city." She swayed. "Why are they just telling me this?"

"They can't feel you. Your thought patterns slide under their notice."

She nodded. "Oh, they are not very nice." One of the men had been in the teashop, and he was having thoughts about her that she wasn't fond of. Oddly enough, in his mind, her hair was long and hung past her waist. His kink was not her problem.

"Those who raid are generally not pleasant people. Do you have all the details?"

She cleared her throat. "More than I would like."

"Excellent. Now, open your eyes and tell me what you saw."

She opened her eyes, and she was kneeling across from Lekorh with their hands touching. "Was that real?"

"It was. It was a guided scan. You took a physical location and settled your mind in that place. When you were there, you found other minds. When are they going to enact their raid?"

She dragged in a deep breath and tried to pull her hands back. He held her loosely but firmly.

"Tomorrow. There is a concert tomorrow in the central park, and they are going to take the women after they have been aroused by the music. Wait, is that a thing?"

He smiled and nodded. "The singers that we invite have an effect on humans that relaxes your inhibitions."

"Cheaters."

"We try to stack the deck in our favour, as you would say."

She snorted. "Right. So, they are taking the humans that they snag to Rohadda. Where is that?"

"It is a particularly unpleasant location."

Sarah wrinkled her nose. "That explains why everything is underground but the portal. Their entire warren of habitation is under the surface."

She looked at him. "Didn't you get this while I was there?"

"No, I kept my mind from you so that I would not taint your experience."

"What?"

"They would have known I was there."

"Oh." She remembered what he had said about frequencies. "How did you know I was sensitive before this happened?" She pointed at her head.

"I could tell by the way you acted around Isabella that

you were reading emotions, and when I began to flirt with you, you broadcasted in sharp jolts."

She blushed. "What was I broadcasting?"

"Surprisingly frank images of me. I was flattered and then fascinated."

Sarah tried to get her hands free. "Right. I think this exercise is over."

"For tonight, perhaps. I will contact Iktabi, and he can notify the Hunters."

"Aren't you going to arrest them?"

"No, we will wait and intercept them. Do not worry, none of your kind will be removed from this world."

"Why not just grab them?"

He nodded and said, "Close your eyes."

She closed them, and the world spun around her, leaving her nude and standing in the teashop. "It's empty."

"Folks who don't want to get caught don't spend much time in one place." Lekorh put his hands on her shoulders.

"Why the teashop?"

"It is central and temporarily abandoned. It was easy to get in and have their meeting and then disperse."

She nodded, and they were back in his quarters. Sarah swayed and clung to his hands.

"Oh, I shouldn't have pushed you." He stood and pulled her to her feet, walking with her in his arms before he set her at the edge of the bed. He pulled her dress off and tucked her in.

She blinked at the rapidity of the procedure but lay back and settled her head on the low pillow. A bit of rest seemed just the thing right now.

Lekorh finished his report to Iktabi, and he waited for a response.

"Are you sure?"

"I was touching her mind as it happened. She was reading thoughts that weren't hers. It is going to occur tomorrow. Can we locate the portal?"

"With the information you have provided, yes."

"Sarah managed the information extraction. I am entering that in her training file."

"We will have Hunters on the alert. Do we know what kind of females they are targeting?"

Lekorh shook his head. "I am guessing that it will be women who have edged toward receptivity during the concert."

"Right." Iktabi frowned. "Do you think we should give them a concrete target?"

Lekorh knew what, or rather, whom he was referring to. "If you can get her mate's cooperation, she might be a way to control their sphere of interest."

"Right. I will ask him." Iktabi sighed and then smiled. "Take care of your new recruit. There are too few of you out there as it is."

"I am registering her as a companion. It will remove the possibility of her being removed from me by the administration."

Iktabi cocked his head. "Is it like that?"

"It is. She is not receptive, but when she is, I will be there."

Iktabi nodded. "I understand. Will you be here to help monitor the events tomorrow?"

"Of course. We will both be there." Lekorh chuckled. "She already has the clearance, but I will have to arrange for some more specific apparel."

"Ah, right. The companion's garb. That is going to take some adjustment. Use the breast support that Argo's mate is so enthusiastic about. Are you going to have her trained as a bodyguard?"

"It is traditional, but I don't think it will be necessary." He smiled.

"You might want to go through the motions, just so as few people as possible know what she is."

Lekorh nodded. "Very well. I will tutor her myself."

Iktabi grinned. "It is a long time since you were a Nool guard. Do you think you can manage it?"

Lekorh snorted. "I am sure I can keep one step ahead of her if I focus."

"You will have to. She is highly intelligent and very used to utilizing her skills for survival. Just make sure that if anything goes awry, you let me know. It would never do for other projects to know that I lost a naturally born psychic."

"She will be my responsibility."

"Yes, she will be. Now, get some rest, you look like you could use some time in bed." Iktabi's words sounded like they carried innuendo, but they were a simple observation of Lekorh's issues with keeping his body rested enough that his mind could work.

Across the Rrassic colonies and projects, the Saya were confined, kept in chairs or centrally located facilities to aid their scanning of the world under their care. Lekorh had despaired when he had first transformed into a Saya. Until the third eye appeared, he had been able to pretend that it was not happening. Once his mind opened, he was assigned to a master and acted as his companion, running errands and being his hands and feet. His master sat in a chair with his mind open, and he searched through every secret and truth in Lekorh and those under his care.

Lekorh decided very early on that he didn't want that kind of life. He liked his limbs under his control, wanted to feel the sun on his face, and even his third eye appreciated the alteration between silence and thousands of minds pushing in on him.

His position in the VIP building, away from the city itself, was a blessed relief, and it was going to make his time with Sarah even more precious. It was just them unless they chose to venture into the city.

Lekorh sighed and stepped away from his desk, stretching and then deciding that he needed to set up a bit more furniture. He had a permanent guest, and making her comfortable was fairly high on his priority list. There was plenty of space, so a few places to sit and relax were in order.

A low chime rang, and he walked to the delivery slot. It was far too early for the furniture, so he smiled as he noted that Sarah's clothing had been delivered. He gathered the small bundle together and carried it into his room where his wardrobe opened as he approached. He hung up her tunics and leggings, folding her undergarments and tucking them into a drawer. His robes took up far more room than her collection of serviceable clothing. When she had her companion wardrobe, he would need another unit added onto this one. Their clothing would hide their fatigue and give them an aura of aloof menace. The Rrassic found him more menacing than humans do. The humans did not know his purpose.

With her clothing put away, Lekorh removed his own trousers and the long hooded vest that he wore when he knew she would be around. She was fascinated with his upper torso, so he made sure that when she was due to come by, he wore as little as he could. He wasn't sure why she was enthralled by his master's markings, but since she was, he used them to increase her fascination with him at every opportunity.

Naked, he slid into bed next to her and let his body cycle toward sleep. He didn't have the sex appeal of the Zjin, the confidence of the Regiz, the power of the Dorbin, or the dark surety of the Luthin. He was a Saya, and he had to use his mind to win the attention of his lady, so he was paying very close attention to what she wanted in a mate.

When he had finished training her and it came time for her to choose a male, he desperately wanted it to be him.

CHAPTER SIX

Sarah woke up in the dark of the night just before dawn. Her body knew it was time to go to work and her mind couldn't override it.

Lying on her belly with her left hand extended, she was surprised at the warmth beneath her fingers. She opened her eyes, and the limited light in the space showed that her hand was linked with that of Lekorh. He was holding her hand as he slept.

Her heart thudded in her chest as she stared at his sleeping features. She didn't want to pull her hand away, but she needed to use the restroom. His third eye opened and began to glow.

She blinked and stared at it, but it wasn't looking at her. She eased her hand from Lekorh's carefully before tiptoeing away to attend the call of nature.

When she returned to the bed, she tried to get back into the same position, but she couldn't manage it.

There was a sigh from the other side of the bed, and his left arm reached out to pull her against him. "Stop fidgeting."

She stiffened and kept her body rigid for a moment, but he was just rubbing her back, and she slowly relaxed. A few more hours of sleep might be just the thing she needed to get herself back under control.

Lekorh used all his training to keep his body from reacting

to her proximity. She smelled sweet, and it was a scent that was all hers.

He held her close and felt the trust slowly grow. Her body relaxed and softened against him, her curves creating a torture that he had never imagined. His inner thoughts were wildly chaotic, but he kept his body calm. He smiled with the chin resting on top of her silky hair. Normally, it was the other way around.

They could spare another hour before they needed to rise to get to the admin building, but that was an hour that he could hold her, so he would not pass it up.

The sooner that Sarah got used to physical contact with him, the easier their linking would be. If they could get to a position of trust, he could see through her eyes, and she would be able to see through his. It was a state that was whispered about by Saya-Rrassic, and for the first time, Lekorh realized it could be more than just a legend told to them to keep them looking for new worlds and new populations to blend with the Rrassic. The chance to find one's ideal match and have it be a complete partnership was a golden prize that was dangled in front of all the Rrassic warriors. The Saya could just see it when the match was true.

A handful of matches were in process across Imrahl at that very moment. The males and females were getting closer to meeting in a circumstance beneficial for them both. The concert later that day should shove a few of them into receptive relationships. He knew that his would not be one of them, but he had time.

Sarah woke to an empty bed. Lekorh's side wasn't even warm.

"Get dressed and come and have breakfast." The words rang in her mind.

She got out of bed, walked over to the lav and washed her face before taming her hair.

Her eyes had dark circles around them but nothing that some tea couldn't cure. She realized when he said get dressed, he had given her some information that she hadn't noticed. Her clothing had arrived.

She went to the wardrobe and opened it, finding her clothing hanging neatly next to his. She chose some dark grey tights with a three-tone grey, gold, and black tunic.

Her underwear had been neatly folded, and that is when she had known that no bots had collected and forwarded the clothing. They moved it and placed it exactly as it had been.

Sarah smirked. She was living with a neat freak.

Once she was dressed, she walked to the main chamber and saw a few changes. The table was now a narrow rectangle, and plumper ones had replaced the simple cushions. There was also a vid unit in one corner with a two-seat couch facing it.

The service set was also different from the one they used the night before. The teapot was larger, the water decanter was larger, and the platters were twice the size.

"Am I going insane or is everything here bigger?"

Lekorh smiled. "With a new companion here, it is only appropriate that I provide for you."

He was wearing loose and comfortable trousers, low boots, a simple tunic, and the hooded robe that marked his position as Saya.

"But how did I not wake up?"

"I deepened your sleep while I was moving things around."

She blinked. "Can you not do that?"

"You needed the sleep. Your brain is still rerouting the signals around the damage."

Sarah sighed and took the platter he handed her. She had

never had scrambled eggs on a formal platter before, but the small strips of toast were welcome. She had no idea how she was going to manage with the eating tongs.

He smiled and brought the tea and water over with him. "You will manage."

She wanted to snipe at him for reading her thoughts, but the food smelled great.

She settled the tray and then knelt on the new cushion.

Lekorh was pouring tea for them. "The eating implements, please."

Sarah got back to her feet and got the chopsticks with tiny claws at the end and a palm plate for each of them.

He grinned. "I don't need the plate."

"I might; I would rather not have to change my clothing again."

She set one plate down to the side and put the other plate on her left palm. She handed him his prongs and inclined her head. "Thank you for cooking."

"You are welcome. So, why don't you cook? I know you can."

She shrugged and picked up a wobbling piece of scrambled egg. She held the palm plate under it and guided it to her mouth. The egg melted, and she was smiling happily. "Because other people do it better. I just like to eat and go."

Lekorh sighed. "Here I was hoping I could get out of the chore."

"Why don't you use a dispenser?" She smiled as she continued to eat the delightfully soft scrambled eggs. She had very little grasp of what animal had laid it, but as long as it wasn't Sthik-Rrassic, she was fine with it.

Lekorh coughed and put his free hand over his mouth. "That is an appalling thought."

She grinned. "I was just checking to see if you were listening."

"I will always be listening unless I am working on a security issue for the city."

Sarah nodded and loaded a piece of toast before lifting it to her mouth. It was acceptable to eat bread products with clean fingers, so as long as she was holding bread, she was good.

"What else did you manage while I slept?"

He continued to eat and then answered, "I contacted the overseer, and he is preparing an action against the raiders who have come in search of humans."

"Good. So, what are we doing today?"

"We are going to the administration offices, and I will go about my day with you assisting me."

She blinked. "What will that entail?"

"You doing research, studying, and meditating. Throughout the day I will ask you to perform different tasks."

She chuckled. "I will have to get you lunch."

"If the food is nearby and you go with an escort." He gave her a stern looked with his gold and silver gaze.

"Right. Wait, why?"

"Because yesterday, you were a high-functioning empath, today, you are a telepath. Now, you are an asset that the colony worlds could and would kill for."

She wobbled her palm plate. "That is an exaggeration."

"I live in the most secure point of the entire world. Another Dorbin-Rrassic could be found to take over, but I am far rarer than Iktabi is. They need me to keep the project moving forward and monitored."

She frowned. "But, Itkabi is in charge?"

"Yes. He deals with the people; I keep my mind open for the issues in the population and report it to him."

"Isn't Iktabi a friend?"

"He is and has been for years, but if he were transferred, I would still have a job to do."

"Right. Of course." She inhaled and nabbed the last bit of egg from the plate. With the last morsel gone, she collected the plates and implements and took them to the sink. There was a dishwashing unit, but it was faster to just scrub them by hand.

She finished the washing up in a few minutes and dried the cutlery and the platter. When the rest of the dishes were clean and put away, she smiled. "So, are we going?"

He beckoned to her and gestured for her to sit. "We are going to sit and meditate for a while. Get used to it. Calming your mind and getting it ready for controlled application is half of our day."

She sighed. "Fine. What do I do?"

"Drink the tea in four sips."

Sarah looked at him suspiciously. "Is that it?"

"That is it. Not a drop left, no sip bigger than the one before it."

She wrinkled her nose and looked at the small cup. "Right. Let me guess, this is harder than it looks."

"It is. I will be tampering with your perceptions of how much you are drinking."

She thought a number of curse words, and he raised his eyebrows but didn't comment.

She sat and picked up the teacup, holding it in two hands as she took her first sip, paused, took her second, and by the time she got to her fourth, she felt the pressure on her mind. After the sip, there was a teaspoon of liquid left, and she glared at him.

He smiled and poured more tea into her cup. "It is a simple thing, and the worst outcome is a full bladder. Try it again. We won't be entering the city until an hour after dawn."

She tried again and again and again until she had finished off the pot of tea.

She groaned and pressed her head to the table. "I am going to slosh when I walk."

"Yes, but you were successful the last two times."

She lifted her head in shock. "What? I saw liquid in there."

"No, you perceived it. That was the point of the exercise. No matter what you thought you saw, I tampered with your perception. We accept the world our mind sees. It is up to us to work out the correct interpretation."

He smiled. "Now we can head into the city."

She stood up and raised her hand. "Just a minute, I need the restroom."

His chuckle followed her, but she didn't care. She had consumed at least a litre of liquid. Her trip to the city would be hellish if she didn't take care of it.

Deceiving someone's mind seemed like an interesting skill to gain. If she could figure it out, she might be able to slip away to play with friends now and then. Hopefully, she would be a quick study.

CHAPTER SEVEN

Sarah felt naked as they got in the lift to get in the compartment on magnetic rails.

"It is strange. You left as one person, and you are returning to the city as something different. Do not worry, I will help you with your blocking when we approach the buildings."

She nodded and wiped her hands on her leggings. "So, how does this thing move?"

"It is a direct shuttle for authorized personnel only. It follows me, and now us, from one site to the other."

"How did Iktabi and Isabella get home?"

"They probably flew. Dr. Lem took this shuttle back to the city, and it returned here when he disembarked."

She nodded. "Okay, so if I needed to return for whatever reason . . ."

"I added your authorization as a resident to the file. It will take you back to our quarters."

Sarah decided to take a leap. "Can I have my own quarters?"

He gave her a wry look. "No. Your official designation is as my companion, so to make sure you can have the freedom that I can manage for you, you must remain with me."

"What does that mean?"

"It means that instead of being classified as a telepath in your own right, you are designated as a sensitive who can assist me with mental overload."

"Do you suffer from that?"

He smiled. "No. But I have found a fit for me and chosen a companion, so you are protected as an extension of my office."

"Oh. Right." She blinked. She hadn't considered that attaching to him might be a form of protection.

"You will also have a wardrobe change, but clothing has been ordered."

"I am familiar with the procedure. I delivered the outfits to the Breeder compound."

"Ah, right. Your courier work. Would you prefer to ride your cycle to and from the city?"

Their cubicle slowly halted, and the doors opened. She gave him a wry look. "Not until I figure out how not to drink all the tea."

He laughed as they left the tube area and walked to the lift that would take them to the upper levels.

When they stepped out and walked to his offices, she peeled away and headed for the restroom. His laughter continued down the hall.

She sighed and finished her business in the restroom. It was a benign training method as far as it went. Punishing a telepath wouldn't have a good result, but making their body annoying was something to be avoided. It was a pretty good tool.

Sarah washed her hands and smiled as she felt Isabella and Iktabi enter the building, buzzing from early morning sex. Sarah quickly walked down the hall to Lekorh's office before the other two could make it to the admin floor.

She might have been a little wild around the eyes when she got into the office and closed the door, leaning against it and feeling like she was being pursued.

"You get used to it. We are on this world, and all the humans are slowly cycling into a mood to mate with the Rrassic. The Rrassic are simply waiting for the authorization from the females." He tapped the side of his head as he sat at his desk. "It is noisy up here."

She nodded. Minds were waking up all over the city, and a lot of them had sex on the brain. When they started doing something about it, she had to take a seat and close her eyes.

The psychic noise stopped suddenly. Lekorh was sitting in front of her, and he leaned in to kiss her, curving a hand around her neck.

She closed her eyes and leaned in, seeking out his mind and only finding that rippling curtain. Sarah reached out and put her hand on his chest, feeling the thudding of his heart. At least he wasn't faking it. His body was reacting just as hers was.

He leaned back, and she grabbed the edge of his vest, pulling him back to her. She felt his surprise, but he deepened the kiss.

When she started to feel the minds around them getting closer, she touched his neck and slowly pulled her fingers away. He leaned back with his third eye blinking sporadically. He didn't apologize, he smiled.

She smiled back and licked her lips to get the last taste of him. His third eye flashed brightly.

He straightened. "Right. We should get to work. You get us tea, I will start the morning sweeps and reports."

She paused as she stood. "Are you going to keep blocking for me?"

"I could, but I think you would be better off developing your own mechanism to keep them out." He smiled and settled behind his desk. "Do not worry, I will monitor you for any stress."

"Do you know why it is worse today?"

He nodded. "You are healing. As your body recovers, the connections get stronger, and you are hearing more."

"When will it stop expanding?"

"When you can hear all of Imrahl by simply focusing."

She nodded. "Right. I will get the tea."

He smiled. "Thank you."

She exited his office and walked down the hall, slowing slightly when she felt Isabella approaching her.

"Sarah!" Isabella walked toward her with a grin.

"Good morning, Isabella." She inclined her head. "I appear to have changed occupations."

"Are you all right? I mean, yesterday was rough."

"I am fine. How is Vedder's transition?" Sarah paused a few feet away from Isabella.

"I don't know. Would you like me to check on him and find out how it is going?"

"Please. I could intrude on him, but I don't really want to."

Isabella nodded. "Right. Wait, can you actually pick out a mind to find?"

Sarah felt the urge to caution in herself and from Lekorh. "If I am close enough. I was thinking of asking Lekorh if I could go for a visit to the med centre later."

Isabella smiled, and there was relief in her mind. "Right. Where are you off to?"

"Just getting some tea for Lekorh and myself. He is going to teach me a bit about what he does all day."

Isabella nodded. "Good. Come and get me if you need anything. I am pretty sure you remember the way."

"Since yesterday? Yes. Thanks though. This is a little weird."

Isabella took a step backward, and that was the point where the link between her and her mate was apparent. They were not only bonded by affection, but the metal bands kept Isabella from moving out of Iktabi's range. She was incarcerated as a security risk.

"I will see you later, Sarah." Isabella turned and walked

back toward her office.

Sarah exhaled softly and went to get the tea. She had seen the bracelets in action, but the fact that they were an actual tether was a bit of a revelation. Lekorh was going to have to explain what was going on there. Sarah had read Isabella's mind, but since she wasn't actively thinking about the bands, there had been nothing more than acknowledging the summons.

The tea set was where she had passed it a hundred times over the last few months. She set up a pot, put in the leaves, and filled it from the nearly boiling water dispenser. She set two cups on a tray with the pot, and she carried the assembled bits and pieces down the hall with careful and quick steps.

She balanced everything on her left arm and opened the door with her right. All the years of table service were paying off in a strange way.

She set the tea on the edge of his desk and checked the brew. It was just the way Lekorh liked it, so she poured him a cup and removed the tea basket.

The cup was set where he could reach it with his left hand, and she poured one for herself. "What do I do next?"

"Check in on your friend Vedder. Isabella will find out where he is, and you can find out how he is actually doing. To do it, you will have to focus on only him, so this is your first challenge. You have until lunch to find him and learn what you can about his state."

She blinked. "Just like that?"

"Just like that. You can kneel in front of my normal station and do your search. I will arrange a second meditation station for you."

"Thank you."

"If you need assistance, I will help when I can, but I am trying to let you find your current skill level."

"Right. Good plan."

She took a tiny sip of the hot tea, and then, she set it where it was safe, and she knelt down in front of the lit altar. The light was bright, and as she settled, it drew her in. She took a deep breath and stared at the light as she sent her thoughts toward the med centre.

At first, the search was fine, but as the workers got onto their transport to their occupations, her focus was shattered a thousand times per foot.

Sarah kept having to reel herself in in order to expand her mind once again. She did it over and over, trying to force her mind through the tangle of thoughts when she felt hands on her shoulders and a warm wall at her back.

His body surrounded her on all sides, and his mind sent out a thin tendril of thought. She threw her thoughts in with him and followed that tendril to Vedder.

Sarah blinked and gasped at the morass of pain and guilt that was wracking her friend. "Can I talk to him?"

"You can. But it would be better if you eased him with the routine of you standing outside the main admin building today before entering my office."

"I didn't do that."

"I know, but sometimes projecting what folk need to see and telling them what they need to hear sets their mind at ease."

So, with him helping her, she built a scenario about her wanting to contact the med office but being unsure about it. She brushed her hair and made a face in the mirror and then an image of her standing outside the admin building.

"Good. It is all verifiable. Now go."

She nodded and sent the scenario into Vedder's mind. His pain and guilt faded. His amusement at the mirror thing was palpable, and she withdrew from his mind as he focused on dampening his own pain.

She leaned back against Lekorh. "Thanks for helping."

"You did well with the construction. What was the significance of brushing your hair?"

"It was the face that I made at myself in the reflection. It is something that I did in the kitchen to the shining metal surfaces and my distorted reflection. He knows I am fine, and where I am."

"Good. You don't give your affection easily." He chuckled.

"I do not. I know what lies beneath their polite flirtation." She enjoyed the moment of peace before she asked, "What am I taking you away from?"

"Nothing. I was going to ask if you would like to go for lunch and get measured for a new wardrobe?"

She snorted. "Don't you have other stuff to do?"

"There is always time for lunch."

He eased to his feet with a light hop and pulled her up until she was standing.

"It is going to take some time for me to get used to being on my knees all the time." She clapped her hand over her mouth as a mental image of her up on her knees and opening his trousers entered her mind.

"Right. Maybe we should eat something ice cold. I could dump it on my lap." Lekorh chuckled. "Do not get upset. I find your fascination with me flattering. It is reciprocal."

She blushed. "I know. I have gotten flashes that were definitely not me."

He raised his brows. "Really, which images?"

"The one with me draped across your desk. This is the one that I would have thought of." She sent him an image of her wrapped around him, his hands on her butt and holding her so that her face was even with his.

He blinked and cleared his throat. "Yes, I believe that definitely is different from one of mine."

She smiled and flicked a glance below the belt under his robes. "So, lunch?"

He sighed and slid his arm around her waist. "You are definitely going to be a distraction."

She smiled brightly. "Good to know."

They exited the office, and Lekorh stopped by the overseer's office before they left the building.

Iktabi stared at the expression on Lekorh's lips. "You look . . . you are in a good mood today."

Lekorh grinned. "We are going out to the market for lunch. Did you want us to bring anything back for you?"

Iktabi blinked. "Out? You never go out."

"I know. Today, I need to take Sarah out for training. We are working on her blocking out crowds, so having lunch in the market area should give enough stimulus."

Iktabi nodded. "Right. This is unusual. You will be listening for information on the raiders?"

Lekorh inclined his head. "I will. Hopefully, they will soon give up and seek females of another species."

They left the building, and Sarah walked with him, his arm around her back a constant presence. The weird thing was that no one was noticing them.

When the Saya was out and about, everyone knew it. The Rrassic stopped and bowed in respect, but the humans stared. Either way, he was never not noticed.

She blinked. "Why is no one staring?"

He chuckled. "They can only see you. You will be ordering for us, and I will hide my presence until we eat, and then, I will appear to be a Luthin."

She chuckled. "So, talking to you would be weird?"

"You can. They will not take notice. How is the pressure on your mind?"

"Not bad. I am trying to create a fog bank around me. It seems to soften the sharp edges."

"Good. You seem more relaxed." His hand on her back was wide and warm, and as they moved into the market area, she was definitely glad he was there.

Chapter Eight

She put in their order at her favourite kiosk and lifted the loaded tray to carry it to where Lekorh was waiting.

He was particularly interested in eating at the food court. It wasn't something that he was normally able to do. Saya-Rrassic were figures of spiritual significance. Their minds were conditioned to still when they saw him. It made it difficult to get information casually, unless he was looking at everyone in a wide sweep, in which case, pulling out specific data was difficult.

She used her senses to move through the crowd, and most of the Rrassic who saw her coming got out of the way. A sharp whistle got the other roadblocks to shift to the side.

Sarah slid the tray on the table, and she got her eating prongs ready. There was one of all of her favourites and two of his special requests.

She felt him pulling the identity of a Luthin over his own aura, and he grinned. She chuckled. She still saw him with his silvery skin and three eyes.

"On your mark, get set, go." She grabbed some pieces of fried vegetable, stuffed the steaming articles into her mouth, and then, she nipped her favourite bits in the noodle bowl, swallowing and lifting the molten noodles into her mouth.

Lekorh wasn't waiting. He dove into the buffet of hot junk food, and she could feel the happy enjoyment in his mind. She smiled, giggled, and kept eating. His mood was pulling up her mood, and when she glanced around, everybody eating had a blissful smile on their faces.

She paused for a bit of a breather and asked, "So, how often does your particular brand of Rrassic find a mate?"

He paused with noodles in his lips. He slurped them in and started chewing. "To date, I have never heard of one. We have companions, but they are usually male and take care of our needs to allow us to focus on our other work."

She nodded. "Right." That they were sexual companions was implied, though she didn't verify it.

"No, sex isn't a part of it."

She was relieved and sad for him at the same time. "That sucks."

He blinked in surprise. "You think so?"

"Sure. There are tons of therapeutic and emotional benefits to touch and intimacy. It helps to stabilize you."

Lekorh cocked his head. "And yet you don't spend much time in that pursuit."

"It is nice, it isn't necessary. I find knowing what my partner is thinking, or at least feeling, isn't very flattering."

He nodded and got some more snacks. "You have been choosing the wrong partners."

She blinked and chuckled. "I would have to agree. I had a narrow selection spectrum. I took what was on offer."

Lekorh was still feeling around for specifics. "The Zjin have popularity with your people."

"Stripes make me dizzy."

He choked at the image she sent him of the blurry stripes moving over her.

"Luthin?" He waved a hand at himself.

"I don't like surprises."

"Regiz?"

"They want a fuller figure. They consider me to be some kind of female larval form."

His shoulders shook in amusement. "Dorbin is out. He is taken."

"Yeah, and that weird bondage thing they have going creeps me out."

"And the midair matings take some getting used to, or so I hear."

She shivered. "Bleah. I guess I am out of luck unless there is another option that would consider me as attractive and charming."

He grinned. "There may be one."

She held up her hand. "Don't say Sthik. I like them, but they have their own thing going on."

He laughed, and heads turned. "There might be another option."

"Well, I am partial to guys with pretty eyes. The more, the better." She batted her lashes at him.

She felt the cool wash through her mind.

"It doesn't bother you?"

"No. It is just what you are. I don't have makeup, so as long as we never fight over eyeliner, I will be fine with it. I like it when it glows." Sarah let him feel the truth of her words.

He looked a little shy when she replayed their kiss earlier. She didn't even know how she did it, it just happened.

He chuckled. "We are going to have to work on your control."

"We need to work on a lot of things." She sighed.

They worked their way through the rest of the tray, knowing that they had just committed to whatever brand of relationship they could manage given his social class.

She cleared their tray and set it on the reclaim station before returning to Lekorh's side.

"Right. So you mentioned wardrobe?"

He nodded. "You are already familiar with the tailor that is used for specific requests."

"Yoris!" She clapped her hands.

"Correct. Shall we?" He offered her his arm, and his broadcast of Luthin energy got stronger.

She took his arm, and they walked through the market on a delightful first date. Sarah accepted it as a first date even though their circumstances were bizarre.

Yoris looked at her with concern the moment they entered the shop. "Sarah, I heard you were attacked."

She shook her head. "No, I tried to help a friend who was beyond help at the moment. There is no blame."

Yoris frowned. "You are all right?"

"I am. This is . . ." She wasn't sure if she was supposed to expose Lekorh. He did it for her.

"Sarah needs your assistance. Her wardrobe is not appropriate for a Saya companion."

Yoris stared in shock. "A companion? They normally wear only the loose upper vest."

Lekorh smiled. "As tempting as the thought is, I believe one of the new breast bands would be appropriate in the place of a naked torso."

"I will work on something. Sarah, I will need to take your measurements."

She nodded and walked to the back where he did his work.

She stepped onto the scan plate, and he cleared his throat. "I need bare skin, please. The undergarments need to be an exact fit."

She sighed and removed her clothing, looking nervously toward the front of the shop. Lekorh was diverting everyone from entering the shop. She chuckled. She stood with her arms out and shoulders back.

The scanner went up and down in a green halo, past her head and back down. When it was done, she sighed in relief.

Getting dressed while a Nool checked the scan and Lekorh broadcasted a blank shop was a little odd, but when her clothing was back in place, she let out another sigh of relief.

She exited the rear of the shop and went back to Lekorh.

He looked at Yoris. "I am expecting some mock-ups before the design is finalized. She needs to be comfortable at all times."

Yoris inclined his head. "Yes, Saya."

Sarah blinked as her friend's mind went into a calm and neutral state. "Dude, that is just odd."

Yoris perked up. "I will miss the pastries."

She grinned and winked. "So will I. Sommin has a good touch with the recipes though. He is just traditional."

Yoris smiled. "He is going to try some of the human recipes today. Your intercession on his behalf has changed his opinion on the matter."

Lekorh perked up. "That is very good news. I must admit that I was mourning the loss of Vedder and his deft touch with sweets."

Yoris chuckled. "I was always after the savouries. His skills will be a loss to our community. Have you heard how he is adapting?"

Sarah looked to Lekorh, and he nodded. "He is in a lot of pain with the body stretching and rewiring. His instincts are rioting, and he thought he killed me until he was informed otherwise."

Yoris winced. "I can understand his pain."

Lekorh nodded. "As can I. Now, we must return to the administration building for this afternoon's work."

She smiled. "Thanks, Yoris. I trust that you won't make me look like an idiot."

"It would be impossible, Miss."

She inclined her head and took the arm that Lekorh offered her. It was that gesture that caused Yoris's mouth to open in surprise.

They walked back to the administration building with folks simply moving around them. He had wrapped them in invisibility for the moment. She leaned her head against his shoulders in the moment of privacy.

"Is something wrong?"

"No. This just feels nice. A moment alone with the world swirling around us."

He pulled her in close and put his arm around her for the last of the few blocks to the administration building. When they entered and scanned in, the guard jumped in surprise, but they travelled up to their floor and returned to his office.

She had to work on her personal barrier between her and the people around her, and he needed to scan the colony and watch the prep on the sting operation that was going to take place that afternoon during the concert.

Part of her wished she could listen to the alien songstress that was being brought in by the administration, but there would be other concerts to listen to. She could do it another time when she could use her mind to protect herself.

Lekorh's protection was entertaining because it was new. If he weren't teaching her to stand up on her own feet, she wouldn't be nearly as pleased about the situation.

She settled on her knees and decided to check on Isabella. Her friend was doing a lot of the actual admin work, arranging shifts, moving staff, and ordering supplies from the main depot.

While she was a little bit intimidated, she checked on Iktabi, and he was working on the sting operation, making sure that everyone was in place. It appeared that the portal had already been identified, and when the raiders started grabbing women, the portal would be disconnected immediately. They held back their action to make sure that all players were in motion. They wanted to grab as many raiders as they could.

She returned to her focus on pulling in a shield of con-
cealment around herself. It didn't feel any different, but she
tried to hold it and stood up carefully to move around the
room.

Lekorh continued his work without a flicker of attention
paid to her. She bent and twisted, touched her toes, and did
a quiet little dance step, all while holding her shield in place.

When she laughed, he looked up, his gaze going toward
the floor and then darting to her. "Well done, Sarah. Now,
check your physical status and see if you need anything."

She looked down and saw that all her clothing was in
place. He got up from his desk and came around to her as
she realized that he was referring to her having burned
through her caloric intake for the day. He caught her as she
swayed.

"So, this is going to take a bit of keeping an eye on." She
smiled up at him.

"How long were you invisible?"

"Twenty minutes."

He grinned. "In that case, well done. I will get you some
sugared tea."

He lifted her and carried her to the chair that was next to
the window that overlooked the city.

She sat there and stared at the expanse of living beings
that were gathering in the park, and she sighed, taking the
cup from Lekorh when he returned.

"Thank you." She smiled and sipped at the tea.

He crouched next to her. "When your mind reads the
waves, your brain becomes a sort of transmission and receiving station. That station needs power, and it takes it from
your cells. This is why most Saya remain immobile while
working and even while they are on their time off."

"Why don't you?"

"I have always felt the urge to be out in the world, and I

was lucky to find an overseer who would allow me to."

"So, it is a good match then, you being here on Imrahl."

"It is. If I hadn't been here, I would never have met you, and then, where would we be?"

"Well, you would be involved in a more efficient day."

He nodded. "And the women at risk might be swept off-world before we could stop the raiders. You have helped, and you are not even trained yet. Give yourself time."

She quirked her lips in a smile. "I am trying, but I am impatient. It is the same reason I don't cook."

"Other people can do it better."

She wrinkled her nose. "And faster. All I need to do is order it, and it magically appears."

He sighed. "We are going to have to work on your definition of magic."

She sipped at her tea and smiled as she looked out the window. At least she wasn't kneeling on the floor again.

He sat back at his desk. "I rather liked that image."

She spluttered, and he laughed while she recovered. The concert was starting, and she wanted to be down with all the couples and people on the greens.

It could have been a perfect first date.

CHAPTER NINE

Sarah was staring outside until her stomach registered its protest that the sweet tea was all that was offered.

Lekorh tossed her a ration bar.

"Uh . . . gross. I can't eat these. I have tried." Sarah fed him a montage of the twelve times she had tried to eat the bars, each ending with her locked in a bathroom and praying that her digestive tract would stop completely.

"Ouch. Right. Well, this is going against my better judgment, but run down to the market and get yourself something."

"Really?"

"But take a guard."

She felt her shoulders slump. "Ah. Right."

A knock at the door a minute later showed her handler. She grinned. "Eegan!"

Her friend and customer came in with a grin. "It is good to see you safe, Sarah. I hear that you are in need of an escort to the market?"

"Yes. I might also need to lean on you from time to time, but no funny business."

Eegan grinned. "If you say so."

Lekorh spoke softly, "No funny business with my companion."

The Zjin blinked and straightened. "No, Saya. I will treat her with the utmost respect."

Sarah got to her feet and grabbed him by the elbow. "Come on. I am hungry."

Lekorh was chuckling inside her mind, and she could feel the tether he had attached to her thoughts. She was going to be out of sight but not out of mind.

Down on the street, Eegan finally was able to talk again. "I had no idea that you were with the Saya."

"I am not *with* him. I am his companion. He sneaks his thoughts into me now and then. That is all."

Eegan nodded. "That makes sense, but Saya normally choose Rrassic for their companions. I have never heard of one out of species before."

"I guess Imrahl is a world for change; now, help me get to the teashop. I want to see if Sommin has gotten to work yet or if he is recovering."

"The shop is open. The pastries need some practice, but few folks have Vedder's touch."

"I will just have to offer him a critique if he is still open."

Eegan walked with her and offered her his arm when she swayed a bit. "Why the pastries?"

"The highest calorie content in the smallest bites." She smiled tightly.

"The only ones I have ever heard of with that requirement were Saya," he joked and then paused. "Wait. You aren't . . ."

She gave him a look and said, "If I was, would I have been running around getting you guys tea cakes and meat pies in the middle of a crowded market shop?"

He sighed in relief. "Of course not. An untrained Saya would have been driven insane by that point."

She nodded. "Lekorh has his issues, but as the city of Imrahl builds toward a mating frenzy, he just needs another mind to take the pressure off."

"Ah, yes. Have you found a likely Rrassic?"

They walked into the shop, and she chuckled. "No, and if

I have to go everywhere under guard, I probably won't."

He chuckled, and she walked up to the counter, looking over the items on display.

Sommin came out from the back, and he stopped when he saw her. "Miss Sarah."

She inclined her head. "Baker Sommin."

He came around, and to her shock, he gave her a hug. "I am so relieved that you are all right. Are you returning to work?"

She shook her head. "No. I have been reassigned. I am stuck in the administration building now."

He nodded. "Ah. It is my loss. I heard what you tried to do for me, and I am so sorry you were injured."

"I am getting over it. Now, I want to try some of your baked goods. I am in urgent need of a calorie hit."

Sommin grinned and walked her through some of the new items he had crafted that day. He looked down. "I incorporated a few of the recipes that you left for me. You have very neat penmanship, by the way."

"Hand me one of those and pack up a selection of everything you are exceptionally proud of. There are sweet cravers on the upper levels of the admin building."

Sommin's eyes brightened, and he handed her one treat on a napkin while the others were tucked into a box and tied with a string.

She bit through the flaky pastry, and her eyes widened at the cheesecake and fruit filling. She wanted to savour it, but Sommin was looking anxious. She swallowed as quickly as she could. "It's wonderful, Sommin. This is definitely going to be a winner."

She munched down the rest while Sommin's expression flooded with relief.

Eegan looked hopeful.

She sighed. "And can Eegan have one as well?"

Sommin took the last one out of the case. "Here you go. I am so relieved. The Rrassic seem to enjoy them, but none of the humans were in today."

"They get excited on concert days. Next time there is a concert, put together small quartets of treats in travel boxes and thermal carafes of iced fruit-flavour sweet teas. The humans will beat a path to the shop."

Sommin grinned. "Excellent. May I consult with you on such matters in the future?"

"Of course." She filled out the bill and swiped her wrist across the pay plate.

Sommin's eyes widened. "I wasn't going to charge you."

She laughed. "That would really have put Vedder into a rage. No, I wanted to come here to see how you were and make sure that business is as usual. It is. Request a server from administration. Having a human female in here makes it less threatening for the clients."

He nodded. "I am beginning to see why Vedder was so insistent that I listen to you."

"If a business that employs me is successful, then that means I have a reliable place to work. That means I have purpose, and with purpose, I have direction. It is all very metaphysical."

Sommin laughed. "Well, come in any time. I welcome your input."

She nodded and brushed the crumbs off her hand. Eegan was holding his pastry like a newborn chick.

She grabbed the box and hung the string from his fingers. "There you go. Guard the pastries."

He grinned, and they left the teashop after she waved at a few of the regulars.

They walked through the market, and to her surprise, the sun seemed to be setting.

"How long were we in there?" She turned to Eegan, but

he was being dragged to the ground.

She opened the senses that she had closed during Sommin's hug, and she was surrounded by Luthin. A hypo to her neck caused her to slump, and a grinning Zjin and a visible Luthin took her arms, holding her up like a limp doll.

They walked her to the edge of the greens where the concert-goers had almost cleared the space.

Eegan was alive but in incredible pain.

Lekorh was furious, and he was on the way.

The gathering of raiders had found their targets, and she was one of them. The other one was a woman with tawny hair and an astonishing figure. She was walking with a Regiz, and she and her mate had an air of competence about them.

When the woman charged the raiders, the two who had possession of Sarah bundled her up and into a vehicle. She wasn't able to do much other than making the driver think he was going faster than he was. She saw a hand groping her thigh and breast through her clothing, but she was literally numb.

They were muttering at each other in High Rrassic. She read their thoughts easily enough. They were taking her to the portal and hoping that their friends could subdue the blonde.

Sarah was limp when the blonde in question ripped past on a cycle. It was a good thing too when Niiva ditched the cycle right in their path. Sarah was held slightly by the groping arm of the passenger. Her head hit the inside of the windscreen, and her body sent a rush of adrenaline that powered through the sedative.

They had stopped. She felt the triumph of her rescuer before her world went dark. They had gotten Niiva, too.

Sarah groaned and was able to press her hand to her forehead. The Luthin next to her was dead. The Zjin was still partially on top of her.

More Hunters arrived, and she grunted and said, "I need to get out of here. She's still nearby, but she can't talk."

She kept hold of Niiva's sleeping mind, but she couldn't get out from under the damn Zjin.

Hands pulled the man off her and helped her out of the vehicle.

Niiva's mate had staggered out of the vehicle next to the wreck. "You saw her?"

"No, but she is here. She is close. She needs help."

She focused on Niiva's shut-in mind. That woman could scream on the psychic plane.

He nodded at her. "Where? Show me."

The other Hunters argued with him, but Sarah led him down the alley with six men following them. She sent a bolt of panic through the man with Niiva. He dove for cover with his prize.

Finding them was simple. The edge of Niiva's boot was behind a stack of boxes. Sarah didn't need to say anything, she just pointed.

There was a rush as the Hunters followed the silent command, and when the Luthin was subdued, one of the Regiz carried an unconscious Niiva out from the spot behind the boxes. Her mate was beyond relieved.

"Is she all right?"

Sarah held herself upright by an effort of sheer will. Lekorh was getting closer, and then, she could relax. "She is. She has been given a paralytic. That is why I could hear her. She was screaming."

The Hunter was relieved that his mate was safe. He and his friends were speaking calmly, and he was bullied into a med transport to get the oozing wound seen to.

Sarah turned and found Lekorh waiting, wrapped in the aura of a Regiz. She walked up to him, and he caught her by the elbows.

"We need to get you to medical."

She felt him rummage through her entire system, and he nodded before he lifted her into his arms. "How is Eegan?"

"He is being repaired. There was no way he could have fought off seven of them."

She chuckled and leaned her head on his chest. "There were six. Typical male exaggerating."

He sighed and said, "I can't even get mad at you. You managed to disable the kidnappers, and you didn't lose your head."

She touched her forehead. "No, but I banged it pretty good. I need to get minimal care for the sedative, and when Niiva wakes up, I will take the repair for my head. She needs to remember who I was and that I am safe. She was fixating on me as a victim, so I need to make sure that she gets closure."

"I am remaining at your side until this is done."

She smiled. "I was hoping you would say that."

She spent the night in the chair next to Niiva, and when she woke up, she reassured the woman that she was well. When Argo was on the way to sooth his mate, Sarah levered herself upright and walked to the door. Lekorh was waiting for her, and he pulled an interesting deception. He stretched his aura to look like two Hunters.

"Nice trick."

He snorted. "I will teach you when you are older."

He took her to the tissue regeneration station for first aid, and her forehead was treated while additional scans were run. She and Lekorh were both relieved to find that no additional damage had been done.

He didn't need to carry her back to the admin building, but he did. He kept her cradled against him, and his mind was comforting but blank for the quick ride.

The lift back to their home was done in silence. She wasn't sure what was going on, but she lifted a hand to his cheek. "Are you all right?"

He looked at her, and his third eye blazed. "I am the furthest from all right that I have ever been."

She felt the maelstrom of his thoughts, and she did the only thing that she could do to stop the burning storm in her mind, she passed out.

CHAPTER TEN

A cool compress woke her. She was lying in Lekorh's lap, and he held the compress to her forehead.

"If there were a way to keep you from putting yourself in danger, I would do it in a heartbeat. As it stands, you are not leaving my side until we can find a way to keep you safe." He had control of his emotions and thoughts again.

She grimaced. "You are not apologizing, so I am guessing—"

"That I figured out you triggered it. You were weak, so it didn't take much, but it did delay the conversation for a while." He moved the compress to her cheek and the back of her neck.

She sighed. "I have got to stop getting hit in the head."

He smiled. "Perhaps you should wear a helmet."

"I just need to find someone safer to hang around with." She chuckled.

"You need to stop looking for snacks."

She cackled, and then, she touched her head. "It shouldn't hurt, but it does."

He pressed his lips to her forehead and the pain drained away.

"How did you do that?"

"You learn that in the lessons that come after not getting hit in the head all the time."

Sarah struggled to sit up, and he adjusted his arm around her back, pulling her up so that her head was leaning against his shoulder.

He sighed. "You have no idea what you are doing to me."

"I have a pretty good idea." She was sitting with the evidence throbbing under her thigh.

He snorted. "Not that, though it is on my mind. Telepaths are selfish by nature, or they lose their minds. With you, all I can think of is us. I am no longer alone, and it goes against everything I have learned and had drilled into me."

Sarah thought about it for a few seconds, and then, she squirmed out of his grip, turned to face him, and crawled into his lap facing him. "If you want to not be alone, then I think we should stop simply teasing each other with images."

She went up on her knees, and she pulled her tunic up and off. Lekorh was locked in surprise.

Her bra hit the floor next to her top, and she leaned against Lekorh, rubbing her breasts against his chest. He wrapped his arms around her, smoothing his hands over her back.

She could feel his delight in the texture of her skin, and she slid her hands behind his head to pull him down for a kiss.

He held her tight and stood up, walking to the bedroom in long strides.

They didn't need to discuss things. If she had a problem with what he was doing, she could tell him without words, and it was reciprocal.

He set her down on the edge of the bed and stepped back to remove his own clothing. She worked her shoes off and peeled her leggings and underwear until all she was wearing was the light in the room.

Lekorh gleamed in the light when it was all he was wearing.

He gave her the most thorough look she had ever experienced, and she could see it through her own eyes, which made it more peculiar. She never knew she had a tiny freckle on the underside of her left breast. It was the first place that Lekorh applied his tongue.

She shivered at the wet heat and ran her fingers through his hair. When he wrapped his lips around her nipple and tugged, she threaded her fingers through his hair and enjoyed the surge of lust that the small caress generated.

He took the hint and began a thorough and devastating assault on her senses. Just when she thought that pleasure was inching into pain, he moved and changed his plan of attack.

She was squirming against the sheets and pulling at his arms and shoulders. Her request was in his mind. She wanted him inside her, and she was trying to get him there.

"If you want me inside you, just say so." His voice was clear, but his mouth was between her thighs as he lapped at her clit.

She tried to ask in clear and concise communication, but it didn't come out. He scraped his teeth along the small bud of flesh, and the air rushed out of her lungs. When she inhaled, she heard her voice saying, "Ohpleaseohpleaseohplease . . ."

Lekorh lifted his head and grinned at her, moving to cover her with his cock gliding up her inner thigh until it lodged in the slick folds that he had been teasing.

She wanted to close her eyes to savour the sensation of him slowly sliding into her, but his third eye was glowing, and it held her hypnotized.

She gasped when he started to press into her. The cool touch of his mind on hers didn't have any effect on the fire in her blood. She lifted her hips to take him deeper, and he slid in another inch.

The dance started so slowly that she wasn't sure if there was a beat at all. She raised her knees and tilted her hips to keep him inside her.

His mind was sending her the feeling of her body gripping his, and the quiver in his mind made her smile and gasp as he thrust deep. He wasn't as sanguine about this as he had seemed.

She pulled him down so she could kiss him, and when she bit his lip, the instinct took over, and they rocked together. Sarah closed her eyes at the feel of him sliding in and out of her.

The feel of him moving inside her was wonderful now that she had gotten used to the girth at the base of his cock. The heat and friction were amazing, but she needed something more.

He leaned to one side while his butt flexed as it thrust. Lekorh slid his hand between them and stroked her cit. It must have been awkward, but there was no indication in his thoughts that this was anything but pleasurable.

He stroked her clit, and his hips quickened their pace. The velvety soft caress of his hide on her breasts added to the sensations, and within twenty strokes and endless circles, she felt fire explode along every nerve. She gasped and shook under him.

Lekorh waited her orgasm out, and then, he pursued his own.

She wrapped her arms around him and drew her nails down his back in a slow pull that ended with her cupping his buttocks and forcing him into her. Her body's rhythm was still pulling at him in slow, pulsing grips.

He growled, and the sound caught her by surprise. He thrust deep and held himself inside her, his hips slowly grinding against hers.

She held him close as his heavily muscled arms slowly collapsed and his body rested on hers.

There was lazy satisfaction in his thought. *"That was so much more fun than simple fantasies."*

"I am very glad it was fun." She smiled.

"Oh, it was. In fact, so enjoyable that I want to build up a library of memories."

She smacked him on the arm. "I am not going to be just a memory."

He lifted his head and smiled down at her. "You don't understand."

To her appalled amazement, he replayed her orgasm in her mind, and her body was triggered into spasms once again.

She shuddered and sucked in air as the cascade of sensation hit her. When the waves stopped running through her, she looked up at him with a dazed expression. "Well, hell."

He grinned. "I am guessing you didn't know I could do that."

She saw the promise in his gaze to repeat the moment as often as he could. "You had better wait for socially appropriate moments to do that."

He grinned. "I will."

She got the distinct impression that he wasn't going to keep it to appropriate times. There was far too much delight in his surface thoughts.

She shifted under him, squirming slightly as she was still impaled on him. His gasp and the flash of enjoyment in his mind were clear, so she did it again and tried to remember what his mind felt like at that moment.

He lifted up on his elbows and kissed her slowly.

Sarah leaned up and into his kiss. He tasted her slowly and deliberately, and she tasted herself on him.

He began to slowly rock into her with controlled arches of his back and thighs.

She wrapped her legs around his hips and undulated with him. It was a delightful forever before her orgasm came over her in a slow and wonderful wave. He withdrew from her when her last internal clasp had ceased, dropping onto the bed beside her and cuddling her against him.

She sighed when she put her right palm between both of his. Being surrounded by heat was relaxing even if the sweat drying on her body cooled the exposed parts.

"I am very glad that we are able to be in contact tonight. Being away from you last night was torture." He murmured it against her temple.

"We were holding hands when I woke."

"I know. My control lapsed somewhere after three in the morning."

She sighed. "No need for control tonight. Is it okay if I just go to sleep? It has been an eventful day."

He held her close and kissed her temple. "Sleep, I will watch over your dreams."

Sarah trusted him, and Lekorh was as good as his word, he watched over her until it was time for breakfast. After breakfast, all hell broke loose.

CHAPTER ELEVEN

Sarah was sitting at the meditation station that had been set up for her sometime between her leaving the previous day and that morning. The cushion was extra puffy, and her focus was a light that cycled through the visible spectrum. She sat with a cup of tea held in her lap, and she focused on letting her mind drift in a slow sweep through Imrahl. From the distant farms to the folks below in the admin, she checked on them all, and none of them had any untoward thoughts.

Lekorh was surprisingly quiet on the psychic plane. There was something that he had to do, and he was trying to keep it from her.

He ran his morning reports, and then, he stood up. "I am stepping out. Remain here."

Sarah stared at him and shook her head. "No. I am going to stick to you today unless I am not authorized."

He sighed.

She could see that he wanted to argue the authorization, but she already had it.

"Fine. Come with me and do not speak. I am going to be interrogating the raiders from last night."

She stood up. "I am going with you."

To her surprise, rising from kneeling was much easier than it had been the previous day. Sure, her thighs were shaking, and there was a definite ache in muscles that hadn't been used in a long while, but all in all, she was having a pretty good day.

He gave her a long look, but he nodded. "Fine, but don't interfere."

She nodded. "I won't."

Lekorh pulled his hood up as they walked the halls and took the lift down to the fifth floor and stopped. "Remain outside the interrogation room."

She nodded. There were two Sthik standing outside a door, and she guessed where the prisoner was currently being held.

"I am going to have to tear his mind apart to get to the information, so protect yourself."

"Yes, Lekorh. I will keep myself calm."

He nodded. "I am counting on it."

She understood that this was a serious matter when he didn't give her a pat or peck or anything. He simply opened the door, and she felt the mind on the other side freeze in panic.

Sarah took up a position across from the door and tried to keep her mind calm and concealed so that she didn't distract Lekorh.

The raider inside was a Luthin, and after five minutes with Lekorh, he was sobbing and curled into a ball, asking for forgiveness.

Lekorh emerged, and the guards half carried, half walked the man out.

Sarah blinked and watched Lekorh key in information through his tablet. "What now?"

"Now, I go through the surviving six. There is a tea station down the hall if you need it." His mind was cold, but she guessed it had to be. He had to remain completely and absolutely calm while going through the raider's mind and picking out the information he needed.

She nodded and remained across the hall from the interrogation room for the next four Luthin and Regiz. She didn't flinch from feeling Lekorh tear one man into every fear he had ever had, and he offered him one way out, tell him what he wanted to know.

Lekorh got the names and coordinates of thirteen colony worlds where stolen females were being used to start new populations. The section of the Rrassic that were doing this thought that there was no chance against the coming invaders, so they were hiding in pockets of time.

Sarah filed that information for later but kept her outer mind calm against the screaming of borderline madness from the other side of the door.

The last interrogation of the morning was the trickiest. She was standing in the hall across from the interrogation room door when the Zjin that had been in the vehicle with her during the crash was led down the hall.

His head lifted as he scented her, and he gave her a leering grin as he was led into the interrogation room. His mind was replaying his enjoyment of her scent and the feel of her through the clothing that she had been wearing.

Sarah hoped for his sake that Lekorh wasn't listening, but she knew he was when his mind when white hot as Lekorh closed the door behind them.

Sarah waited for a few minutes when the questions were being asked, and she knew the moment when the Zjin opened his mouth regarding her.

The heavy thud of bodies hitting the wall was unmistakable. The two guards turned and tried to open the door, but one of the bodies was wedged up against it, and that body was suffering the punishing impact of fists and teeth.

Sarah saw through the Zjin's eyes, and her calm Lekorh wasn't the one that had just finished a report in the hallway. He was beyond rage, and he wasn't going to stop until the male who had enjoyed hurting and groping her was dead in the throes of terror and agony.

Sarah sent her thoughts to him, calming him and sending him the memory of her arms being wrapped around him. She wasn't trying to hold him back, but she was trying to keep him from killing someone during the interrogation. It was the sort of thing that could get someone removed from a posting.

She felt a flicker of response from him, and the heavy, wet sound of a body being pulled away from the door was audible through the barrier.

The Zjin was lying in a spreading pool of blood. His guards grabbed him and pulled him out of the room with only a quick glance to the other inhabitant of the interrogation chamber.

Sarah walked in, stepping over the bloody smears on the floor. She blinked at Lekorh's appearance, but she smiled at him. "I am fine. He didn't hurt me. It was embarrassing at the time."

Lekorh had two large fangs that were covered with blood, as were his fists and the front of his robes.

She chuckled. "I am pretty sure I would have noticed those teeth last night."

He blinked. She was replaying the moment when he was lying on his belly with his face between her thighs.

"They retract. Most Saya don't need them."

"Most Saya don't mate." She stroked the blood on his cheek and shared her concern for him.

He sighed, closed his third eye, and pressed the upper edge of his forehead against hers. "I don't regret it."

"I only worry about how it will affect you."

"It won't. We are a population colony. Defending your mate is expected, no matter who you are."

She wrapped her arms around him, the scent of blood and the blood itself getting on her clothing. "Just so you know. I feel the same. If anyone tries to injure you in any way, they are going to be in for a very bad time."

He chuckled and held her close.

Iktabi appeared in the doorway. Sarah could feel him staring at her back. "What happened?"

Sarah mumbled, "The Zjin shared his thoughts and plans for me, continuing the groping from last night into a fully formed fantasy."

"Ah. Right. Lekorh, change your clothing. We have a meeting this afternoon."

Sarah smiled as the overseer left. "Well, that was unexpected."

He chuckled. "I did tell you, we are a population colony. If there is a chance that I can be the first Saya in generations to have a child with a new species, he will take credit for it as the Overseer of Imrahl."

"He takes credit for your reproductive capability?"

"No, for my grace and charm. Come on. We will return home and change."

She grinned and parted from him, covered with half the blood of the Zjin. "A shower might also be in order."

"I had heard that ladies were fussy, and you are definitely holding to the rumour." He grinned, and his canines had retracted, both sets. The upper and lower teeth were a little surprising, considering his urbane appearance.

They walked to the lift and headed down and to the private shuttle.

He held her on his lap and nuzzled her neck on the short ride to their home. Sarah blinked when she realized that part of his libido was being driven by the scent of blood. She kept that bit of observation to herself.

Sarah started peeling off her clothing in the lift and walked out of the transport into their home, carrying her clothing and boots.

She felt rather than heard Lekorh behind her, and he lifted her and carried her into the bathroom, as naked as she was.

The water struck her back, and she wrapped herself around Lekorh like a spider monkey. He turned to get the water jets between them, but she kissed him, blocking some of the spray. He turned and pressed her back against the wall, letting the spray rain down on them from that angle.

She was having fun, and his mind was calming from the fury that he had experienced earlier. Sex was an amazing distractor.

When he pried her off him and washed the blood from her, she made a face. He washed himself from top to toe, and she wrapped herself a drying cloth. He stepped out and dried himself off.

She turned and walked into the bedroom and toward the wardrobe. His arm caught her around the waist, and he hauled her to the bed while her mind cackled in triumph.

"You are incorrigible." He sat on the bed and settled her on his lap facing him.

She stroked a hand through his damp hair. "You looked like you could use some stress relief."

She wrapped her free hand around his cock and pumped slowly. His eyes closed, but the third one kept a narrow-eyed look on her with his lashes quivering slightly.

She grinned and kissed him, nipping at his lower lip. She kissed her way down his chin to his neck. The muscle flexed as she gripped it with her teeth, and she kept moving downward, sliding off his lap until she was kneeling on the floor.

His mind was tense, and he replayed the image she had sent him of her on her knees in front of him over and over.

Sarah trailed her fingertips up his inner thighs and back down again as she leaned toward him, feathering warm breath over the head of his cock. He was tense, and she kept her mind blank so that he couldn't see what she was doing a moment before she did it.

Close examination of his cock showed her velvety dark-pewter skin, a nearly charcoal-coloured cock head, and the vaguely conical shape that the Rrassic were designed so that they fit in a variety of orifices. If the head fit, they could get in anywhere.

She leaned in and wrapped her lips around the dark head, stroking his shaft with one of her hands in a light but firm grip.

He groaned, and a quick look upward showed her that the only eye he had open was the third. She suckled as she pulled back and breathed in and out via her nostrils as she worked him, taking him closer and closer to the edge.

Her own pleasure was riding on the back of his, and she felt the heavy throbbing between her thighs as she continued to suck and stroke.

He came to a decision, and she only had a moment before he carefully detached her from him, and then, he lifted her to the bed on her hands and knees at the edge of it, he stepped between her thighs and slid his cock into her without any hesitation. She was so wet he went in easily, and as he began to thrust deep into her, he reached around to stroke her clit in a quick and furious frenzy.

She groaned, grunted with the impact, and whimpered from the assault on her clit, finally letting out a low guttural cry that accompanied her body trying to shake itself apart while gripping him tightly.

He gripped her hips and grunted as he pounded into her, against the subtle clasp of her muscles. She listened for the signal of his impending orgasm, but her body flared suddenly, and a second round of trembling and shaking took her over, with bright images burning behind her eyes.

Lekorh groaned and shoved into her hard, his hips pressing spasmodically as he thrust against her. She could trace the outline of his pleasure, but her own was getting in the way.

He chuckled and ran his hand down her spine. *"There will be other days, Sarah, other memories."*

His body shook as his cock spilled into her again. He collapsed on her, and his weight took her to the bedding.

She sighed and relaxed, snuggling into the sheets under him. He was finally relaxed and in a good mood, and she was delighted to have been able to help since she was the issue that had gotten him into the protective rage.

"You were not. He made a choice to pursue you without your consent. I have to say, I have rarely seen a Zjin so surprised."

She sighed and tried to turn over, but he kept her there, placing a soft kiss on her cheek. "I want you to stay here while I finish the meetings this afternoon. We are going to be discussing the future of Rrassic-human offspring with the women who have their foetuses in the canisters. I do not think that it is a situation you can contribute to, and you may be a distraction to Niiva. She needs to focus on what she wants to do as her first two samples have just entered gestation."

She blinked and looked for why, finally nodding. "You don't want my opinion of the matter coloured by the ideas of others."

"Yes, and the humans don't know that you are the Saya-human. We are trying to pretend that you are simply my companion, or as your folk think of it — sex-slave."

He pressed another kiss to her neck and levered off her. She had pretended outrage, but instead, she moved to his side of the bed and crept under the sheets.

She wondered if there was a wet-spot with the Rrassic, and she was just malicious enough to find out.

He got dressed, and she realized that he was going into a

room with mated Rrassic and humans, and he smelled like her. The humans might not know, but their mates would.

Lekorh went in in a far better mood than he had left in, and though she had pretended to be going for a nap, she was filled with energy.

A quick shower took care of the minor amount of cum that had leaked out, and what had emerged seemed to absorb into her skin. The scent was similar to Lekorh's, a light musk with a strange spicy contribution.

She went to the terminal and checked her correspondence. A note from Yoris was there.

I thought you should see the designs before he makes the choice for you. I am voting for the third as formal wear and the others as day wear.

She opened the attachment, and she blinked. "Well, at least I am going to have a bra of sorts."

The clothing consisted of loose trousers that tied around the waist, a breast band that was held in place with straps that were rather pretty, and a long vest with a hood.

She sent Lekorh the query about which one he liked. It was fun to be able to annoy him while he was in a meeting.

When they finished their fast-as-thought discussion, she went to order her clothing, and he knew what a stripper pole was and how it was used.

The free exchange of information was rather fun, and she looked forward to doing it for an extended period of time. Preferably locked in the bedroom with a supply of snacks.

CHAPTER TWELVE

The clothing parcel arriving was a lot of fun. Lekorh was trying to meditate, and she kept jostling him out of it for the fashion show.

He gave up and watched as she switched between the bras and trousers, mixing and matching them with the vest.

He smiled. "Do you know why we wear the open vest?"

She shook her head. "There isn't much on Saya in the accessible archive."

"We wear our status marks on our chest. When you gain journeyman status, it would be traditional for you to begin your tattoo. When you become a master, it would be increased to this level. If you manage to gain the title of ancient, your entire chest is covered with designs."

Based on his previous day's activities, she asked, "What if we get pregnant? Is there a tattoo for that?"

He grinned. "No, but we could make one. Right now, your breast band is fine, but as your tattoos are created, the fabric will minimize."

She turned from side to side. "So, what is the significance of the vest?"

"It shows the marks and lets folks know that we are not combat troops."

"The hood?"

"Hides the eyes. There is still an impression of them when folks look at us. The third eye is a link into the psyche of the Rrassic, so our kind are trained to look for it."

"And it is easier to get into someone's mind if there is no

eye contact."

"That as well."

She chuckled. "So, how did the stripper pole go over?"

"She requested three more so that she can teach classes." He smiled hopefully. "Are you interested?"

Sarah raised her eyebrows. "Am I allowed?"

He thought about it. "Perhaps we could get one installed here, and she could teach you privately."

She grinned. "She probably would."

Niiva was as open-hearted as she was open-minded. Sarah had been able to move through her thoughts with ease and nudge them in a way that made her uncomfortable but kept Niiva from knowing exactly what she was.

"Have you done your scans today?"

She gave him a dark look. "Yes."

"Do them again and tell me what you find. There is something new happening, and you will need to attend to it."

She wrinkled her nose and stalked to her meditation station, flicking her robes out around her in dramatic fashion.

She looked at the cycling colours and let her mind drift free, looking for anything out of the ordinary.

She went through the minds rapidly, looking for anything strange and then remembered that he had said new. She focused on the gestation facility, and her eyes went wide. "The baby is coming out."

He chuckled. "Yes, she is. I have notified the facility and Iktabi as well as the parents. In the future, I am making this one of your tasks."

She nodded. "Wow. That is so cool. Are they on their way?"

"They will be there within the hour. Put on your formal clothing as this is an auspicious moment that will be recorded and sent back to our headquarters."

She smiled and got up, heading back to the wardrobe and

removing the elaborately embroidered clothing that was her formal garb.

She stripped, and to her surprise, he did the same. They got dressed side by side, fixed their hair, and then, she was next to him in the lift.

"This feels very tense to me."

He nodded. "It is. Bree is an accelerator. Her child developed at an abnormally fast rate, which means that she could build an entire colony on her own as long as she had medical assistance to remove the embryos."

"Do you think we will have children?"

"It is unlikely, but it is possible. Saya usually occur naturally in the population, but I have been unable to find a record of them being bred between the Rrassic and another species."

They got to their pod, and he entered a new destination.

"It takes us straight to the gestation centre?"

"It does. We are already under security protocols, so there is only going to be one checkpoint inside the facility."

She nodded. "Okay. Good."

She was nervous. She loved babies. Their emotions were always so raw and honest. There was very little that they could do that would upset her, and they were completely harmless if slightly messy.

"So, they are going to be taking her off-world?"

"They are. She will be raised with others as they come due, and her parents are being encouraged to procreate as rapidly as they can to get a step up on our population."

They were whizzing along the new line, and she simply tracked her location via the thoughts of those above her. "Is there an ideal number?"

"Twenty thousand warriors are what we are looking for."

"Interesting number."

"That is the point at which we mobilize and join the

Rrassic defense forces. Until then, we are personnel supply."

The pod stopped, and they disembarked.

"Right. Got it." Sarah lifted the hood of her ankle-length vest, straightened the front, and smiled at the Saya next to her. He geared up as well and nodded.

It was time to go formal, and she was prepared to play at being the companion.

They were scanned and verified before they were allowed into the gestation centre, and from there, they were escorted up to the floor where the canisters were held.

Lekorh murmured, "We are the first ones to arrive."

Sarah nodded and moved around the space under the watchful eye of the attendant.

The baby who was making her debut was in a canister that was glowing with blue light. The tiny mind was excited because the people around her were excited. She was going to meet the parents who had read her stories and sang songs to her and the others in the gestation tubes.

Sarah was amazed at the awareness of the tiny specks that surrounded her, but it must be like a baby crying in a restaurant. Once one went off, the others followed.

The baby was sucking on her fist in the snug confines of the cylinder. She had enough room to move, but just enough.

Lekorh walked up to her and placed a hand on her shoulder. "We need to step back and wait. The parents have arrived."

The next half hour was spent standing slightly behind Lekorh as the excited humans gathered respectfully with their mates for the tremendous honour of being there to see the first human-Rrassic hybrid draw breath.

She saw Niiva and her mate standing near the others, and she didn't wave. Keeping her face neutral was tremendously difficult.

She watched the baby slide out of the tube and the medics quickly taking care of the umbilical connection.

"The canister massages the umbilical cord and pumps all the blood into the infant in a mimicry of the action of a live birth."

"That is neat. You guys have put a lot of effort into making healthy little ones."

"The mortality rate for humans in delivery is unacceptable, so it was determined that all pregnancies should be removed from the host and placed in the canisters. It is safer for the women."

"Safer, but there are those who would want the experience."

"We will deal with that issue once our population has met expectation."

Sarah didn't nod, but she sent him a murmur of understanding as Bree held her daughter for the first time.

There was a moment of tense silence, and then, the child let out a wail that turned into a bellow.

"It is her war cry. She's a fighter." Sarah fought her grin.

Lekorh's mind was startled at the sound. He had expected the soft sounds that he associated with infants.

She played him a track of the worst infant wails that she had heard over the years. He blinked slightly and remained at his post.

Iktabi and Isabella walked over, and they admired the new addition to the population, the others all walked over and congratulated the trio.

When most of the folk had wandered off, Sarah stepped around Lekorh and walked over to Bree, Arix, and little Remi.

"Congratulations, she is beautiful and very smart. She is going to be a fierce fighter."

Bree looked at her. "Didn't you used to work at the tea-shop in the main market?"

"I did. I am now companion to the Saya."

Arix straightened. "It is an honour to meet you."

Sarah smiled. "It is my honour to be here today. Remi is

going to make waves in our society."

Bree grinned. "I think so, too."

Sarah reached out and paused. "May I hold her?"

Bree dumped Remi in Sarah's arms.

Sarah grinned and turned to Lekorh. "I don't think he has seen one of these up close before. I will be right back."

Lekorh met her halfway, and he touched the baby's cheek. "She is silver and pink."

"I am guessing that it is the combination of Rrassic and human genes. Maybe her body will go through a Nool phase."

He looked at her in surprise. "Our females do not."

"Yes, but this is a whole new being. She thinks you are shiny."

He sighed and tickled the baby's chin. "I know."

Sarah grinned, and she returned to the parents who were discussing leaving Imrahl with the baby and most of the canister library. Producing the hybrids was about to go into high gear. The handoff was swift, and Sarah returned to Lekorh's side while the overseer and his mate discussed the situation with the new parents.

Sarah looked at the occupied canisters and thought about the future of the Imrahl population-generating colony. The children were going to start coming fast and in large quantities. She hoped that the Rrassic were braced for it.

Lying in Lekorh's arms that night, she smiled. "It is too bad that it is unlikely that we can make a child."

"It really is. I would love to see if we could make a daughter with our mixed genes."

"Not a boy?"

"The Rrassic can make males. Making a sane female is far more difficult."

Sarah's shoulders shook as she laughed. "I would say that

it comes down to a stable environment, no matter how wild the girls get."

"So, having Bree and Arix with her will be helpful?"

"Very."

He sighed and pulled her close. "Good."

"Would you go to raise your child?"

"I could not, but I would definitely send you to an accelerated world to raise them."

She smiled slightly toward the night sky. "I am still not sure how the time bubble dimensions work."

He started to explain it, and before he got around to letting her know that she would only be missing from Imrahl for a week while she and the child lived out twenty years. She was asleep before he got to the child's third birthday.

As a sedative, there was nothing like a temporal discussion to get the melatonin firing.

Watching the transport being loaded with all of the canisters with current embryos was another ceremonial moment. Sarah stood next to Lekorh and watched as the flying unit filled with canisters was activated and moved toward a portal at the port.

The parents of the gestating little ones waved them off, and Bree, Arix, and Remi were off to the creche world. With the incursions of raiders, it was safer for the next generation to be beyond reach until they were grown. Regular shipments of embryos and new human and Rrassic caretakers would be sent out.

Sarah rubbed at her neck and waited until the flyer was gone and the portal was closed. There was a support team waiting for them, and it was a good thing. Sarah hoped that when her little one was sent to the creche that there was someone like Bree on the other side, taking care of her.

Lekorh looked at her sharply. "What?"

She smiled at him. "Nothing. I just need to check something at the med centre."

He stared at her in shock. She remembered how he had looked that morning with his canines extended as he bit down on the join of her neck and shoulder. Stimulated ovulation occurred in certain species on Earth, but she hadn't given much credence to it until the chemical reaction started inside her and her senses were keen enough to pick up on them.

The ballet of biology and chemistry that was occurring inside her was fun to think about, but keeping it from Lekorh for the last four hours had been a personal test.

"Wait. You are serious. You think you are pregnant."

She didn't have a chance to answer, he picked her up and spun her around before he set her on her feet and kissed her passionately. She was up on her toes with her arms wrapped around his neck when Iktabi came over.

"Lekorh, is there something amiss?"

Lekorh lifted his head, and he smiled. "I believe that we have unprecedented news, but it needs to be confirmed."

Iktabi suddenly got excited. "Really?"

Sarah looked at him with a bland expression. "Pretty sure on my end, but let's get an official consensus."

Twenty minutes later, the scan told her what she knew. She had started something or, rather, someone.

Lekorh was in shock and held her hand, pressing kisses to the inside of her wrist. He held her hand as the cell cluster was extracted, and once the life had been transferred to the canister, a light came on, and the canister glowed yellow.

The medics looked at each other, and Sarah could feel the mental high-fives.

The tiny cell cluster was sent under very serious guard to the gestation centre. Development would have to be verified, and that would take time. She would develop at half the pace of the other babies if she developed at all.

Sarah and Lekorh were going to have to wait.

They were sitting together, alone in their private space, and Lekorh was still shocked. "They are going to have to report this if she lives."

"I know."

"They may want to try and replicate you."

She wrinkled her nose. "I guessed that much from your line of thought."

"Is it odd to think of yourself as being replicated and shipped around the other colonies?"

Sarah leaned her head against his chest. "Unless they cloned you as well, they might have no luck. The Saya that they put in their path will have to be exceptional to even be in your league."

He chuckled. "I wonder if they will have the nerve to crack her skull."

"I doubt it, but I am not worried. The ladies will have the good sense that my genes gave them, and hopefully, empathy will be the first thing to manifest. If you have empathy for those around you, you can do amazing things."

Lekorh chuckled and sent her a wave of warmth. "Speaking as one of those amazing things, you can do me whenever you like."

"That is how we got here to begin with."

They laughed together and then made plans to monitor their offspring. They wanted the little female to survive and thrive, but time would tell. In the meantime, they had each other, and all the memories that they had made . . . together.

Author's Note

Book 5 is behind me and now book 6 looms. Lekorh and Sarah have gained the attention of the Rrassic council, and that means an emissary is going to arrive on Imrahl.

Hint. It is a species we haven't seen yet.

Thanks for reading,

Viola Grace

ABOUT THE AUTHOR

Viola Grace (aka Zenina Masters) is a Canadian sci-fi/paranormal romance writer with ambitions to keep writing for the rest of her life. She specializes in short stories because the thrill of discovery, of all those firsts, is what keeps her writing.

An artist who enjoys a story that catches you up, whirls you around, and sets you down with a smile on your face is all she endeavours to be. She prefers to leave the drama to those who are better suited to it, she always goes for the cheap laugh.

In real life, she now is engaged in beekeeping, and her adventures can be found on the YouTube channel, Mystery Bees Apiary. Just look for the cartoon kittens.

www.ingramcontent.com/pod-product-compliance
Lightning Source LLC
Chambersburg PA
CBHW070510130626
46555CB00003B/1240